THE MAN OUTSIDE

Working abroad, John Fordyce and his sister returned to England after learning that John was the beneficiary of the estate of his uncle, William Grant. Taking up occupancy of Raven House, a large mansion in its own grounds, they engaged servants to run it. But soon a series of mysterious events followed. A man was seen lurking around the house, and there had been an attempted break-in. Then the chauffeur was found in the library — stabbed to death . . .

DONALD STUART

THE MAN OUTSIDE

Complete and Unabridged

LINFORD
Leicester

First published in Great Britain

First Linford Edition
published 2013

A catalogue record for this book is available
from the British Library.

ISBN 978–1–4448–1690–7

Published by
F. A. Thorpe (Publishing)
Anstey, Leicestershire

Set by Words & Graphics Ltd.
Anstey, Leicestershire
Printed and bound in Great Britain by
T. J. International Ltd., Padstow, Cornwall

This book is printed on acid-free paper

11857802

1

The House

The house stood on the fringe of a wide expanse of rolling moorland; had stood there in its setting of trees for centuries. It had started as a humble cottage, had been pulled down and rebuilt with a piece here and a bit there added by each successive tenant until it had lost all semblance to its original form, and become a gaunt edifice of crumbling stone whose only pretension to beauty lay in the ivy which mercifully softened its harsh and ugly line.

When William Grant bought it, it had been empty for over five years, for no one apparently relished the idea of living in this desolate spot surrounded by the bleak wind-lashed moor, and within sight on a clear day of the great convict prison at Princetown. But the old man, for reasons of his own, had welcomed the solitude it offered, and was not dismayed by the neglected appearance of the wooded grounds or the dilapidated condition of the house itself. Under his direction the fine old drive, with its avenue of beech trees, had been cleared of the weeds and rank undergrowth that choked it. The old panelling and floors within restored and repolished, and the whole place made habitable and put into some semblance of order.

William Grant was sixty-three when he bought Raven House, grey-faced and grey-haired, with features as rugged as the crags and tors at which he loved to gaze from the upstairs windows of his home. A lonely man who seldom smiled, and who neither saw nor spoke to anyone, except the elderly couple who attended to his few wants. For two years he lived there peacefully among his books and his flowers, for he was a lover of both, and then the accident happened which for a time at least, rendered the old place once more tenantless. No blame was attaching to the driver of the car, as the coroner was most careful to point out at the subsequent inquest. He had done his best to avoid running down the old man, by swerving sharply as he stepped unexpectedly into the roadway. But Grant had tried to save himself by jumping backwards. The whole weight of the car had gone over his neck, and death had been practically instantaneous.

He was buried after the usual preliminaries in the little churchyard at Tor Bridge, and the only mourners at the funeral were his two old servants, and the solicitor who had come down from London to take charge of his affairs.

He had left no will, and his property, which was considerable, including the house on which he had spent so much care and trouble, went automatically to his nephew, who was also his next of kin.

John Fordyce was in Canada, holding down a not too lucrative job as accountant in a canned fruit company when the news of his uncle's death reached him, and he immediately gave in his notice, packed his belongings and came to England with his sister, Peggy, a slim, fair-haired girl, ten years younger than her brother.

Their parents had died five years

before, within six months of each other, and curiously enough, from the same complaint, double pneumonia. The children, left practically penniless and with no friends to keep them in England, had drifted to the colonies, and eventually to Canada, where John had succeeded in securing the job at which he was still employed when he received the news of his good fortune.

It came as a complete surprise, for he had only seen his uncle once, at the funeral of his mother, and had completely forgotten his existence until the solicitor's letter recalled it to his mind. But his surprise at finding himself his uncle's heir was as nothing compared with his surprise at the amount involved. When he went into the old man's affairs, he found, to his astonishment, that he was not only well off, but a very rich man. His uncle had had property everywhere; a block of flats here; a row of shops there. Whole streets of houses in prosperous suburbs; a large interest in a Welsh coal mine and innumerable holdings in substantial companies. The income from all of these totalled up to the enormous sum of nearly a hundred thousand pounds a year.

'I'd no idea that the old boy was as rich as this,' he said to the round-faced solicitor, when the amount was made known to him. 'How did he make his money?'

The jovial Mr. Homer was vague.

'He was a very good business man, Mr. Fordyce,' he said evasively. 'All his investments were of the soundest.'

'But what was his business?' persisted John curiously.

The solicitor shook his almost bald head.

'I don't know,' he replied with a little dry cough. 'He never told me, and he was not the kind of man with whom one could force a confidence. He had, I believe, an office in Upper Thames Street for some years, but what he did there' — he shrugged his shoulders slightly — 'I haven't the least idea.'

'Well, whatever it was, it must have been very profitable,' said John, and the solicitor agreed.

His first sight of the house that was

now his was rather unfortunate, for it was in the pouring rain, and a thin, damp ground mist swathed the moor in a chilling blanket. The whole place looked so desolate and dismal that he viewed it with mixed feelings.

Peggy, rather to his surprise, was wildly enthusiastic. The rugged grandeur of the moorland scenery fascinated her. The long line of russet and olive slopes broken with great glistening boulders; the majestic tors and crags; the little huts of stone, relics of a forgotten people, that dotted the hillsides; the space and immense breadth of it, left her a little breathless and wondering.

'Jack, it's marvellous!' she said with shining eyes. 'I guess I'm just longing to move in.'

John Fordyce was more than a little doubtful.

'It's not bad,' he answered rather grudgingly. 'A bit bleak, don't you think?'

'Bleak!' her voice was scornful. 'I think it's wonderful! Just imagine what it would be like with the sun shining.'

'I wish I could!' retorted her brother, as

a cold raindrop trickled down the back of his neck. 'Let's go and see what the inside of the place is like.'

When he had seen it he was less disparaging. Old Grant had had his own ideas of comfort, and had spared neither trouble nor expense in carrying them out. The rooms were all beautifully furnished, and in spite of the dust, which had accumulated while the house had been shut up, presented an air of cosiness, which was very pleasing. The bedrooms, of which there were seven, were all fitted with hot and cold running water, and central heating had been installed throughout. Internally the place was as modern as the latest block of flats in the West End of London.

'It's a lovely house,' said Peggy when they had explored every room and cupboard, 'and it's just the right size. Not too large and not too small.'

'In fact, ideal!' said John Fordyce, in full agreement with his sister's verdict.

They moved in the following week after a rather strenuous time. There had been servants to engage and many things to buy; clothes and a heap of odds and ends that their newly-found prosperity made possible. There is a joy in spending money for the sheer love of spending that few people can resist, and they exploited this to the full.

It was during one of her shopping expeditions that Peggy met Frank Elford again. It was surprising that he should have recognised her, for they had not met for over six years, and when he had last seen her she had been all legs and hair; a girl in her teens just crossing the line which divides childhood from womanhood. Frank, himself, at that period, had been a lanky youth with a snub nose and freckles, and a predilection for a particularly virulent kind of sticky toffee. The freckles still faintly remained but the snub nose had become more shapely, and there was, Peggy noticed rather thankfully, no trace whatever of the toffee.

He was surprised and delighted to hear that they were remaining in England, and insisted upon coming down to see them at their new home as soon as he could snatch the time from his paper. He was, he told her, crime reporter on the *Morning Sun*, and unless any special news 'broke', was due for a holiday in a fortnight's time.

Apparently no special news did 'break', for he arrived at Raven House in the early hours of a sunny morning, and announced his intention of staying for a couple of days. John Fordyce suggested that he should make it a week but Frank shook his head.

'I'd like to, but I can't,' he said. 'I must go and put in a few days with an old aunt of mine. She's as deaf as a post, and thinks I'm still about six, but there are expectations, and business comes before pleasure.'

He was enthusiastic about the house, and its setting, and spent quite a lot of his time in rambling about the moor with Peggy.

It was with very real regret that he took his leave.

'I'll come down again as soon as ever I can,' he promised in answer to the girl's invitation. 'It's a wonderful spot and I think you're both awfully lucky!'

John Fordyce went with him as far as Exeter, where he had an appointment to interview a new chauffeur. The man's references were satisfactory, and John liked his appearance and manner. He engaged him on the spot, and came home by train.

It was on the following morning that the letter arrived. It was addressed to Peggy, and the girl read it with a puzzled frown.

'Did you know we had an aunt Georgina?' she asked looking across the breakfast table at her brother.

John put down his newspaper and shook his head.

'Well we have!' said Peggy, 'listen to this:

'My dear Margaret,' she read aloud, 'I feel I must write and congratulate you and John on your good fortune. I expect you will remember your Aunt Georgina, who used to take you out for walks when you were quite small. I should so much like to see you and John again, and, with your permission, I propose to come down and spend a few days with you both. Eustace — I don't know whether you will remember him but he was about your own age — has not been very well lately and the country air will do him good. Of course, if this should be inconvenient, please wire. Unless I hear from you, I shall be leaving for Devonshire tomorrow morning. Yours affectionately, GEORGINA YAPP.'

'Tomorrow morning means today,' said John Fordyce frowning. 'Georgina Yapp.' He puckered up his lips thoughtfully. 'I seem to remember the name.'

He reached over, took the letter from Peggy's hand and read it through again.

'By Jove, yes!' he exclaimed suddenly. 'I do remember her! Of course! She was a friend of Mother's; a dreadful woman!!

Peggy looked at him in dismay

'Well, what had we better do?' she asked. 'Send a wire, and tell her she can't come?'

Her brother rubbed his chin undecidedly.

'It seems unkind to do that,' he said at length. 'I believe she was very good to mother.'

'Then we'd better let her come,' said Peggy, 'and Eustace, whoever he is.'

'He's her son,' replied John. 'He must be about your age, now. So far as I can remember he used to be a skinny little fellow; an awful prig.'

'How nice!' remarked Peggy wrinkling her small nose. 'It looks as if we are going to have a good time!'

'I don't suppose they'll stop very long,' said John, hopefully, but in this he was to prove a poor prophet.

It was at ten o'clock that evening that the visitors arrived in the ancient Ford, which plied for hire at the little station of Tor Bridge, and Peggy, with a sinking of the heart, saw that they were accompanied by sufficient luggage to suggest that their stay might be of long duration.

Georgina Yapp was a tall, thin woman of masculine appearance, which was enhanced by her closely-cropped iron grey hair, and the monocle which she wore screwed into her left eye. Her voice was deep and booming, and she greeted John and Peggy with a handshake that would have done credit to a navvy.

'You haven't changed much,' she said curtly, 'and looked appraisingly round the hall. 'Nice place! Grant always did know how to make himself comfortable! Where's that fool son of mine?'

She strode over to the open front door and glared out.

'Eustace! Come here!'

Eustace, who was fussily superintending the unloading of the dilapidated taxi, turned obediently and came hesitantly up the steps. He was a weedy youth of rather less than medium height; his sallow face pale and unhealthy looking. He held out a limp hand to John, and smiled at Peggy in rather a sickly fashion.

'It's perfectly delightful of you to have us,' he said, and his voice was high, with over stressed sibilants. 'I'm sure it's going to be very nice here.'

John caught sight of the expression on Peggy's face, and coughed violently.

'I'll go and help the man to bring in your luggage,' he said hastily, and went out to the assistance of the aged driver.

By the time they had succeeded, between them, in getting the array of trunks and suitcases into the hall, Peggy had carried away the guests to show them their rooms. John paid off the cab, and was turning away from closing the front door when she came down the stairs.

'Well?' she said, and there was dismay in her eyes.

'Well?' grunted John. 'How long are we expected to put up with those two?'

The girl made a grimace.

'From the amount of luggage they've brought,' she nodded at the pile in the hall, 'it looks as if they'd decided to stay for some time.'

Apparently she was right, for the days passed and Georgina Yapp and her son showed no signs of leaving. They neither mentioned nor even hinted at the possible date of their departure, and eventually John and Peggy became resigned to the inevitable. They could think of no satisfactory excuse for getting rid of them, and so far as Georgina was concerned, when they knew her better, they came to like her in spite of her brusque manner and blunt speech. It was Eustace who got on their nerves. His mincing way of talking and affected, effeminate manner exasperated John almost beyond endurance, so that at times he found it difficult to avoid being openly rude. Curiously enough, this dislike was apparently shared by Georgina, for she treated her son with the greatest contempt, and never missed an opportunity of holding him up to ridicule.

Eustace certainly was a little trying. He was under the impression that he had been born a poet of genius — why, after having heard some of his lyrical efforts, neither John nor Peggy could understand — and was subject to moods, which he explained were due to his artistic temperament. When his mother pointed out that they were much more likely to be caused by liver and lack of exercise, the expression on his face would have been envied by one of the early Christian Martyrs. In spite of Eustace, however, they found it very pleasant at Raven House. Life on the edge of this vast open moor was very peaceful and satisfying, and John, who loved the country, found fresh cause for delight with every passing day.

It was not until they had been living there for nearly three weeks that they received their first hint that life at Raven House was not going to be quite so peaceful as it seemed.

2

The Man

It was Nellie the kitchen maid who first saw the man.

She came running back to the cook in terror with a white frightened face, and sobbed out her story almost on the verge of hysterics.

'Stuff an' nonsense!' snorted the stout Mrs. Docker. 'You bin readin' them thrillers. Men with masked faces indeed! You're crazy, girl!'

But Nellie persisted in her story.

She had a young man who lived at Exeter to whom she was in the habit of writing long letters. Just before dinner she had gone out to post one of these at the mailbox, which was fastened to the wall a few yards down the road from the entrance to the drive. The night was very dark and she had borrowed the chauffeur's electric torch to light her way.

Coming back to the house she had slipped and stumbled halfway up Beech Drive, and the torch had fallen from her hand. As she picked it up its light had focused on a patch of shrubbery at the side of the drive and it was then that she had seen the man.

'He was tall an' thin an' gaunt-like,' she described him to the cook graphically, 'an' 'e was dressed in a funny shiny black coat. 'E 'ad a soft hat pulled down low over his eyes, an' his face was covered with some sort of black stuff. 'Orrible, he was!'

'What was he doin'?' demanded the cook.

'Just crouchin' there,' answered Nellie. 'Give me a fair turn, it did!'

She had recovered from her first shock, and was rather enjoying the unaccustomed position of being the centre of interest. But Mrs. Docker was still inclined to be sceptical.

'I don't believe there was anyone there at all,' she declared shaking her head. 'What you saw was a shadder or a funny shaped bush, an' you imagined the rest.'

Nellie became obstinate.

'I didn't imagine nothin',' she said stubbornly and a little indignantly. 'I tell yer I saw this feller with my h'own eyes!'

'Well you couldn't 'ave seen 'im with anyone else's!' snapped the cook. 'Go an' wash up an' don't lets 'ave any more nonsense!'

The only person who really appeared to believe her story was Gore, the new chauffeur. He was a good-looking man on the right side of forty, rather superior to the usual run of chauffeurs, and a great favourite with the rest of the servants. Nellie recounted her adventure to him, later, when she returned the torch, and he listened with gratifying interest, questioning her closely on the appearance of the man she had seen. But she could add nothing to what she had already told the cook.

The story reached John Fordyce through Anne, the housemaid, and he was inclined to be as doubtful as the cook had been.

'Do you really think she saw anybody?' he asked.

'I'm sure she did, sir,' replied Anne seriously. 'Cook still thinks she imagined it all, but I believe there really was someone there.'

She was looking a little nervous and John decided to treat the incident lightly.

'A tramp most likely,' he said, 'and she imagined the trimmings. Of course, all this mask business is sheer nonsense. Anyway, we'll be extra careful in locking up tonight.'

He thought no more about the matter, until two nights later when he saw the man himself.

It had been raining heavily all day, but towards evening it cleared up, and after dinner he decided to go for a walk. The night was clear with a pale moon, and on his way back up the drive he thought he saw a vague movement on his left among the beech trees. Remembering Nellie's experience, he stopped and looked more closely. He had not been mistaken; a dim figure was moving stealthily through the shrubbery. As he watched, it came out into a little patch of moonlight, and he saw it clearly. It was a man dressed in a long black coat, and wearing a soft hat. He could see no face, only a smudge of black . . .

He made up his mind quickly, and leaving the drive plunged into the thickly growing bushes after the trespasser. But by the time he got to the place where he had last seen it, the lurking figure had disappeared. In all probability the intruder, whoever he was, had heard him and had taken fright. John could still hear the sound of his hurried progress through the bushes, and set off in pursuit, but he failed to find the man he was seeking, and although he searched diligently the whole of Beech Drive he saw no more of the mysterious visitant that night.

He went back to the house feeling vaguely uneasy. Who was this man who seemed to spend his time lurking about in Beech Drive, and what was his object? Robbery was the first solution that came to his mind. The house contained many valuables, and John himself kept a large sum of money in his desk in the library. He considered the idea of informing the police, but by the time he had reached the house decided against this. He had no wish to alarm the rest of the household, and for this reason he said nothing about the man he had seen. He did, however, take the precaution of examining all the doors and windows before he went to bed that night, to make sure that they were securely fastened, the burglar theory still in his mind.

There was no attempt to break in, however, during the night, and although John kept a sharp lookout for any sign of the man in the drive during the next three nights, he saw nothing.

It was on the fourth night that a rather alarming incident occurred.

Peggy had been suffering from a slight cold during the day, and went to bed early.

She was some little time falling asleep, but eventually she did. How long she slept, she had no idea, but suddenly she found herself wide awake and sitting up in bed. The room was in complete darkness, for the window was heavily curtained, and there was no sound to account for this sudden disturbance of her slumber, although something had certainly awakened her.

She stared into the darkness for a moment listening and, stretching out her hand, she switched on the small table lamp by her bedside, and looking at the dial of her little French alarm clock discovered that it was just after three. She listened again. It was raining heavily outside and the drops were pattering on the window but otherwise all was quiet.

After a second or two she turned off the light, and slid down into the bed with the intention of going to sleep once more.

But sleep would not come. She turned from one side to the other, and at last in desperation, she decided to go down to the library and fetch a book, which she had been reading. She put on the light, got up, and pulling on a dressing gown, thrust her feet into her slippers, and opening the door of her room, slipped out into the corridor.

It was very dark and rather cold, and she shivered as she felt along the wall for the light switch. Finding it she pressed it down, and as the light from the soft shaded electric pendant dispelled the darkness, she made her way to the head of the stairs. There was no sound in the sleeping house, and softly descending to the hall, she went over to the library door and opened it.

A rush of cold, fresh, air greeted her as she crossed the threshold, and she heard a startled oath. Her hand flew to the switch and as the light sprang on she saw that the french windows were open. She also saw something else and the sight drained the blood from her face. A shapeless figure in black was crouching half inside the room. It turned its covered face towards her and she screamed.

And then she must have fainted for the next thing she remembered was John Fordyce bending over her and forcing brandy between her trembling lips.

'What happened?' he asked anxiously as she struggled up from the settee, on to which he had lifted her. 'What made you scream?'

Rather shakily she told him, and his lips compressed.

'I thought it was something like that,

when I came down and saw the windows were open,' he muttered. 'What was the man like?'

She could only give a vague description, but it was sufficient to convince John that the night intruder had been the man he had seen in the drive.

By this time the rest of the household had become alarmed, and Georgina and Eustace put in an appearance, the latter clad in a wonderful dressing gown that looked like Joseph's coat of many colours.

'What's happened?' asked Georgina screwing her monocle into her eye. 'Who broke the window?'

John explained, and the grey-haired woman raised her eyebrows.

'If you'll look after Peggy,' he ended, 'I'll go and ring up the police.'

'How delightfully thrilling!' murmured Eustace with a little ecstatic shiver.

'You go back to bed!' snapped his mother harshly. 'You'll only be in the way!'

'Oh, but really, Mater — ' he began to protest weakly, but she cut him short and eventually he had to obey her. He had reluctantly left them when John came back to say that the police were arriving as soon as possible.

Georgina went out to the group of frightened servants clustered in the hall, and ordered hot coffee. When she came back John was making a careful examination of the french windows. A small circle of glass had been cut out near the latch, and through this the burglar had put in his hand and drawn back the single centre bolt. John found the circle of glass that had been cut out on the path outside; attached to it was a piece of treacle-covered brown paper, which had been used to prevent it falling inside the room and making a noise.

On the face of it, it looked like an ordinary attempt at burglary. The man he had seen in the drive had probably been watching the house for some time in order to spy out the land and get acquainted with the habits of its inmates. John had read somewhere that this was the usual procedure.

Anne, looking very white and frightened, brought in the coffee, and they drank it gratefully. They none of them felt like going back to bed, and when a fire had been lighted in the drawing room, they sat round this and discussed the alarm of the night.

It was not until eight o'clock that the police, in the persons of an inspector and a constable, arrived.

Inspector Jukes was not by any means an imposing individual. He was a big man, with a fat, unhealthy-looking face and a drooping sandy moustache that almost concealed an unusually small mouth. His little pig-like eyes blinked continuously, as though he suffered from weak sight, which in fact he did, and his hair was thin and plastered down on his flat head. When he spoke it was in a deep bass that seemed to come from his stomach.

He displayed a vast amount of energy, examined the window and the path beyond, wrapped up the piece of glass and treacle-covered paper, and asked innumerable questions, while the constable with a very grave face made copious notes.

They were there for an hour altogether, during which time Nellie related her experience twice, John three times, and Peggy until she could have repeated it word for word by heart. At the end of this time Inspector Jukes scratched his head, remarked gravely that it 'certainly looked like an attempted burglary to him,' and went away with the assurance that he would communicate with John Fordyce as soon as he had any information.

Georgina was inclined to treat the whole thing lightly.

'I don't suppose you'll have any more trouble,' she said. 'This man's made his attempt and failed. He'll know you've informed the police and he won't try again.'

'I hope you're right,' said Peggy.

'Of course I'm right!' retorted the elder woman firmly.

And so the episode ended. John heard nothing further from the police; the glass of the french window was replaced, and the little excitement faded into the background of everyday life, and was forgotten, except by two of the household, until the tragedy to which it had been a prelude burst upon them in all its horror.

3

The Visitor

John Fordyce got up on the morning of that fatal day without any premonition of what was to happen before the night came again. Had he had any warning it is doubtful if he would have whistled so gaily as he shaved and bathed, or have enjoyed his after-breakfast walk quite so much as he did.

The day started gloriously, with the moor bathed in the pale rays of an autumn sun, but after lunch it began to cloud over, and by tea-time the rain was falling heavily; a monotonous downpour that threatened to last far into the coming night.

Gore was taking the car into Tor Bridge that evening to fetch a parcel of books that John had ordered from London, and which he had been notified were waiting for him at the station. He came into the library before leaving on his errand, to enquire if there were any further instructions.

'I don't think so,' said John looking up from his book. 'Unless Mrs. Yapp wants anything. You might ask her.'

The man touched his cap respectfully and took his departure. Ten minutes later John heard the car go down the drive, and the hum of its engine fade away in the distance. He rather liked Gore. The man was quiet and well-behaved, and not only an excellent driver but an excellent mechanic. It was Anne who had recommended him. He had been in service with her before, and when she heard that John was looking for a chauffeur, she had made her suggestion. Just before it was time to dress for dinner, he remembered some letters that he ought to have answered before, and sat down at his desk to attend to them.

This made him a little late, and when he entered the dining room, the others were already seated at the long table. With a murmured apology for his tardiness, he took his place and the meal began.

It was very cosy in the big, oblong

room, with its panelled walls and beamed ceiling, and not for the first time he thanked his stars for the luck which had come to him.

As Anne was serving the fish, he remembered that he had not heard the car return.

'Has Gore come back yet?' he asked.

'No, sir,' answered the housemaid. She looked at him a little oddly and her lips parted as though she was going to add something, but apparently she thought better of it, for she said nothing else.

'What a time the man is,' muttered John. 'He's been gone nearly three hours.'

'Where did he go?' asked Peggy.

John told her.

'Perhaps he's waiting for the rain to stop?' suggested Eustace.

'The rain won't stop tonight,' said Georgina. 'Listen, it's worse than ever. More likely something's gone wrong with the car. A puncture probably.'

'That's possible,' agreed John. 'Let me know as soon as he gets back, Anne, will you?'

The housemaid inclined her head.

'Yes, sir,' she said and left the room noiselessly.

She had just brought in the coffee, when they heard the sound of wheels on wet gravel, and presently the unmistakable squeak of a car's brakes.

'There's Gore, now,' said Peggy, but her brother shook his head and frowned.

'The brakes on our car don't squeak like that,' he answered. 'If it's Gore he's come back in another machine.'

Apparently it was not Gore, for presently they heard the soft ring of the front door bell, and Anne went to answer it. Shortly afterwards came the sound of voices in the hall, and Peggy looked across at John, with a puzzled expression.

'Somebody's called,' she said, 'I wonder — '

'Perhaps it's the burglar,' remarked Georgina fitting a cigarette into her long holder, 'come to apologise for trying to break in the other night.'

'Well, if it is, he can pay the glazier's bill.' said John laughing, and at that moment Anne tapped at the door and entered.

'There's a gentleman to see you, sir,' she announced and John raised his eyebrows in surprise.

'To see me?' he said. 'Who is it?'

'A Mr. Wainwright, sir,' answered the housemaid.

'Wainwright?' repeated John. 'I don't know anybody by the name of Wainwright.'

'He's waiting in the hall, sir,' said Anne. 'What shall I tell him?'

John rose to his feet.

'I suppose I'd better go and see who it is,' he said, and followed the girl out into the hall.

A young man of medium height, whose fair hair gleamed like polished leather under the light, was standing staring up at a picture on the wall. He turned as he heard John approach, and held out his hand with a smile.

'Hello, Puddles!' he said calmly.

John stared at him with an expression of incredulity and amazement that was curiously mingled.

'Good God!' he exclaimed. 'It's 'Stinks' Wainwright!'

'The prefix is superfluous,' said the other, nodding, 'but otherwise you're correct. How are you, John?'

'Well I'm damned!' said John, and seizing the outstretched hand wrung it heartily.

'As bad as that, eh?' said the fair young man sympathetically, his eyes twinkling, 'Well, I can't say I'm surprised, you always gave me the impression that you'd end up that way!'

'How the devil did you get here?' demanded John.

'Some people call it a car,' said Wainwright shaking his head, 'others I must admit have been less polite — '

'I don't mean that,' broke in John impatiently. 'I mean how did you know I was living here?'

'That,' said the other, 'is a long story, and although I am considerably wet outside, I am very dry internally!'

'Which means, I suppose, that you want a drink,' said John. 'Take off your coat, and come into the library.'

The visitor removed an ancient mackintosh, and followed John into the comfortable book-lined room.

These two had been at school together, and the last time John had seen Wainwright had been just before he and Peggy had left for the Colonies.

'Now,' said John when he had supplied his friend with a large whisky and soda, 'tell me all about yourself, and how you managed to dig me out here.'

Wainwright gulped down half his drink and looked at him critically.

'You look disgustingly fat and prosperous,' he remarked, 'but otherwise you haven't altered much.'

'You've changed a lot,' replied John squirting soda into his own glass. 'I should never have recognised you if you hadn't used that old nickname.'

Wainwright drank the remainder of his whisky.

'I've done a lot of things since you saw me last,' he remarked, and then abruptly changing the subject he went on: 'I'm here entirely by accident. I happened to have some business at Tor Bridge when I heard that this house had just become occupied by a fellow called John Fordyce.

The name aroused in me sufficient interest to make further enquiries, and when I was told that you had a sister called Margaret, and that you had both recently come back from Canada, I guessed that you must be the friend of my childhood days, so I took a chance and here I am!'

'And here I hope you'll stop for a day or two at least,' said John quickly.

'If you have any more of that whisky,' retorted Wainwright, setting down his empty glass, 'I most certainly will! You know you're regarded as a most romantic figure in the district, Puddles,' he went on after a pause, 'the heir from abroad and all that sort of thing. I must say you seem to have struck oil. How did it all happen?'

John gave him a brief account of the circumstances of his inheritance.

'Nearly a hundred thousand a year, eh?' Wainwright pursed up his lips and uttered a long whistle. 'Quite a bloated capitalist! Well, I've done a lot of things, but I haven't yet been able to persuade anyone to die and leave me a fortune!'

'What are you doing now?' asked John.

'Nothing,' replied Wainwright, leaning comfortably back in his chair and surveying him through half-closed eyes. 'I haven't long been back from abroad myself.'

He seemed disinclined to talk about himself and John suggested that they should join the others.

'Georgina Yapp is staying with us,' he said. 'You remember her, don't you?'

Wainwright rose lazily to his feet.

'Do I?' he said. 'Wait a minute let me think. Is that the woman who used to snap my head off because I would pull her son's hair?'

John grinned at the recollection.

'Yes,' he answered, 'he's here, too.'

'Quite a happy family,' said Wainwright. 'I'm afraid they won't be a bit pleased to see me, though. They both hated me like poison.'

'Georgina's not so bad,' said John as they crossed to the door, 'her bark's much worse than her bite.'

'Is she still barking?' asked Wainwright with a grimace.

John nodded.

'Just a little snappy,' he replied.

Peggy, Georgina and Eustace were in the drawing room, and their surprise when they saw the visitor was almost as great as John's had been.

He, however, greeted them as though the last time they had met had been yesterday.

'You have improved in appearance,' remarked Georgina, removing her long green cigarette holder from her lip, and eyeing him through her monocle. 'And apparently in your habits! This is the first time I've seen you with clean hands and face!'

'You will have that pleasure for several days to come,' retorted Wainwright coolly. 'By the way do you remember — '

He launched into a string of reminiscences, and was in the middle of these when Peggy remembered her duty as a hostess.

'I'd better see about a room for you,' she said, and rang a bell.

There was a slight delay before Anne answered the summons, and when she did come she seemed a little breathless.

'You rang, miss?' she asked, and John thought that she looked rather white and frightened.

'Mr. Wainwright is staying, Anne,' said Peggy. 'Will you set the room next to Mr. Fordyce's ready?'

'Yes, miss.' The housemaid turned towards the door and then stopped, hesitating, her hand on the knob.

'What is it?' asked Peggy.

Anne looked nervously from one to the other, and then she said slowly:

'The man has been seen again, miss.'

John heard Peggy's quick intake of breath and his eyes narrowed.

'When?' he asked sharply.

Anne moistened her lips and when she answered her voice was husky.

'About half an hour ago, sir,' she said. 'It was cook who saw him this time — from her bedroom window, sir.'

'Where did she see him?' asked John frowning.

'The same place as before, sir,' answered the housemaid, 'lurking among the bushes at the end of Beech Drive.'

Georgina gave a scornful sniff, dropped

her monocle from her eye and deftly caught it.

'I don't suppose it was the same man,' she remarked sceptically.

'Cook swears it was, ma'am,' Anne looked towards her quickly. 'She said he was the same as Nellie described.'

'I wonder who the devil he is?' muttered, John pulling irritably at his lower lip.

'Nellie and cook are scared to death, sir, and I — I feel — a bit frightened, too.'

'My good girl,' broke in Georgina, vigorously polishing her eyeglass with her handkerchief,' 'There's nothing to feel frightened about.'

'Isn't there, ma'am?' said the house-maid, her restless eyes moving from one to the other. 'What about that attempt to break into the house the other night? Wasn't *that* enough to make anyone feel frightened? And then this man in black who's always hanging about the place at nightfall. He's up to no good or he wouldn't wrap his face up so that it can't be seen. There's — there's something horrible about his waiting out there in the wind and the rain. What's he waiting for? That's what I should like to know.'

'You're not the only one who would like to know that, Anne,' said John, and Wainwright who had been listening interestedly broke in:

'Who is this man? What's it all about?'

'It's nothing very much,' answered John and explained. 'Peculiar, isn't it?'

'Very,' said Wainwright, and to John's surprise his face was rather serious. 'Anyway, he can't do much harm, whoever he is, so long as he remains outside, can he?'

It was Anne who answered him.

'No, sir,' she said. 'But it's the — the — noises that frighten me most. *They're* not outside.'

'Noises! What noises?' asked John in surprise.

'The noises in the night,' she answered him a low voice. 'Haven't you heard them?'

He shook his head.

'I've heard nothing,' he declared. 'What are they like?'

'Sometimes they're a sort of muffled

tapping,' explained the housemaid, 'like someone hanging pictures. Sometimes they sound like shuffling footsteps as though someone were walking about in slippers. The other night' — she shivered, and her voice sank to a whisper — 'they came right down the corridor and stopped outside my bedroom door. I thought at first that perhaps somebody in the house wanted me, but when I got up and opened the door — there was nobody there!'

'Nonsense!' snapped Georgina crossly, 'you were dreaming!'

'No, ma'am, I wasn't,' said Anne steadily, 'besides I'm not the only one who's heard them. Cook's heard the noises too.'

'So have I,' said Peggy unexpectedly.

John swung round towards her.

'You've heard them?' he said.

She nodded.

'Yes, twice,' she answered. 'Three nights ago and again last night.'

'You've never said anything about it,' grunted her brother. 'Have you heard any sounds during the night, Georgina?'

'Only Eustace snoring in the next room,' she replied curtly.

'Oh, Mater, I don't snore,' protested her son in horror.

'I say,' exclaimed Wainwright, 'this is really interesting! At what time do these noises start?'

'Generally between one and two o'clock in the morning, sir,' Anne replied.

'But who on earth is likely to be walking about at that hour?' protested John.

'I don't know, sir,' said the housemaid. 'But whoever it is, or *whatever* it is, it's nothing that can be seen.'

John laughed a little uneasily. There was something disquieting in the suggestion that her words implied.

'Do you mean that the place is haunted?' he said.

'I don't mean anything, sir,' answered Anne quietly. 'I'm only telling you what I've heard — and I'm frightened.'

Georgina shrugged her shoulders, and carefully fitted a fresh cigarette into the end of her holder.

'I think you're all making a lot of fuss

about nothing,' she said. 'Old houses make queer noises sometimes, you know. The older the house the queerer the noise.'

Peggy looked at her doubtfully.

'It may be that, of course,' she agreed, 'but after that attempt to break into the house and this strange man who's always lurking in the drive, I'm wondering — '

What she was wondering they never knew, for at that moment there was a crash of breaking glass, as something came whizzing through the window and fell with a thud at John Fordyce's feet!

4

Fresh Blood

Anne screamed, and the others were so startled that for a moment they could only stare in astonishment at the jagged hole in the window.

It was Wainwright who first recovered from the shock, and picked up the object that lay on the carpet by John Fordyce's feet. Balancing it in the palm of his hand, he looked at it with raised eyebrows.

'I wonder who sent you this?' he remarked. It was a large stone, still wet and muddy, and from its condition could only have been picked up a few seconds before it was thrown through the window. John stared down at it frowningly.

'Heaven knows,' he grunted. 'It seems a stupid thing to do.'

'What is it?' asked Peggy, crossing over to him.

Wainwright showed her.

'It looks as if somebody has a grudge against you,' he said. 'Have you discharged any servants, a gardener or anybody like that?'

John shook his head.

'More likely it was a mischievous boy,' said Georgina, 'I can't imagine a grown man doing such a silly trick.'

'I think it's doubtful if there would be any boys round here at this time of night,' said Wainwright. He looked up at John. 'Suppose we go and see if we can find anybody.'

John agreed to his suggestion, and they went out into the hall and put on coats and hats. Stopping to collect a flashlamp from his desk in the library, John followed Wainwright out into the darkness of the drive.

The rain was still falling heavily, and the wind had risen, so that it blew the drops into their faces. They paused for a second at the foot of the steps and listened, but there was no sound except the rustle of the trees, as their branches swayed back and forth, and the patter of the rain on the fallen leaves. The dark tunnel of the drive merging away to shadowy blandness, looked anything but prepossessing, but they were not concerned with this for the moment, and made their way round to the shrubbery overlooked by the drawing room window.

There was no sign of any living thing about. The thrower of stones, whoever he had been, had evidently made off immediately after launching his missile, for there was no trace of him. Before going back to the house they walked down as far as the drive gates, flashing the light on either side and keeping a sharp lookout for anybody who might be lurking in the shrubbery, but they saw no one.

'I didn't expect we should find anybody,' remarked Wainwright, as they came slowly back towards the house. 'There was plenty of time for them to get away before we came out.'

John grunted.

'I'd like to know what the idea was,' he muttered. 'It seems such a senseless thing to do. Unless it was done for sheer wilful damage, I don't see what object has been served.'

Wainwright glanced at him sideways, and in the darkness his face had suddenly gone grave.

'Apparently quite a lot of things have been happening round here that don't make sense,' he answered. 'What about this man in black who's always lurking round the house, and these noises in the night. What do you make of them?'

John shrugged his shoulders rather irritably.

'I don't make anything of them,' he said. 'I've never heard the noises.'

'But you've seen the man,' said Wainwright quickly. 'The noises may be imagination, but he's real enough?'

They had reached the hall by now, and were removing their damp coats.

'Oh yes, he's real enough,' said John grimly. 'There was no imagination about the hole he cut in the library window.'

'I wonder if it was he who threw the stone?' muttered Wainwright thoughtfully and John stared at him.

'Why should he?' he demanded. Before the other could reply, Peggy appeared at the door of the drawing room.

'Did you see anybody?' she asked a little anxiously.

'Not a soul,' answered John shaking his head. 'The place is deserted.'

Anne came out behind her mistress; she was breathing rather quickly and jerkily and her pretty face was frightened.

'You didn't see anything of Gore, did you, sir?' she said, and though she made an effort to speak calmly, her voice shook.

Fordyce started. Up to that moment he had forgotten all about the chauffeur. It was rather curious that the man had not come back.

'Not a thing,' he declared. 'It's extraordinary! Where can he have got to?'

'Who's Gore?' Wainwright raised his eyes with sudden interest.

'My chauffeur,' explained John. 'I sent him over in the car just after tea to Tor Bridge to fetch a parcel of books, and he ought to have been back at least three hours ago.'

'I hope nothing's happened to him, sir,' said Anne, and the tone of her voice showed that her nerves were on edge.

'I don't see what could have,' John

spoke with a conviction he was far from feeling. 'He's an expert driver, I shouldn't think he could have met with an accident.'

'It's not an accident that I'm afraid of, sir,' began Anne nervously, 'it's — '

She stopped and appeared a little embarrassed.

'What?' demanded John quickly.

She opened her mouth, hesitated again for a moment, and then:

'It's the man in the drive, sir,' she answered.

'Good God, Anne,' broke in the loud voice of Georgia Yapp from the drawing room, 'are you raking up that nonsense again?'

She came out into the hall, her long cigarette holder between her fingers, her monocle glistening in her eye.

'I don't know what's the matter with everybody. You all seem determined to make mystery out of nothing at all.'

The housemaid swung round towards her, and two little pink spots came to her colourless cheeks.

'There's no need to make mystery,

ma'am,' she said, her voice hoarse with fear. 'There *is* mystery — the whole house is mysterious, Who is this man who is always hanging about in Beech Drive? Why did he try to get in the other night, and what is it that walks about and yet can't be *seen?*'

Georgina laughed scornfully, and Anne went on quickly:

'It's nothing to laugh at, ma'am, there's something going on around this house that's evil. Something we none of us know about, and the man out there is at the bottom of it.' She swept her hand towards the closed front door. 'That's why I say I hope nothing's happened to Gore!'

She was almost hysterical; on the verge of tears, and Peggy laid a hand on her arm soothingly.

'But why should Gore be in any danger, Anne?' she said gently. 'Why should this man, whoever he is, harm Gore?'

'I don't know, miss,' the housemaid was calmer, but her lips were trembling violently, 'but — well, he — he hasn't come back, has he?'

Georgina sniffed contemptuously.

'Rubbish!' she exclaimed. 'I've never heard such nonsense! I expect there's quite a reasonable explanation. The car has probably broken down.'

'I hope you're right, ma'am,' said Anne, 'but — '

She stopped abruptly as though she had thought better of what she was going to say, and turned towards the staircase.

'I'll go and attend to Mr. Wainwright's room, miss,' she said quietly. 'Shall I light the fire, it is laid?'

'I think — ' Peggy was beginning when Wainwright interrupted her.

'No, please don't,' he said hastily. 'I don't like a fire in my bedroom.'

'I should like you to put one in mine, Anne, please,' the high voice of Eustace floated out through the open drawing room door.

'What do you want a fire for?' snapped Georgina, glaring at him as he came out into the hall.

'I adore a fire in my bedroom,' said Eustace. 'It's so comforting and the warmth helps me to think.'

'Hell itself couldn't do that!' retorted his mother. 'No fire, Anne!'

'Oh, but really — ' began Eustace plaintively, but Georgina interrupted him.

'You heard what I said, Anne,' she rapped sharply. 'No fire!'

'All right, ma'am.' Anne turned and went up the stairs, and Eustace sniffed disgustedly.

'It'll be your fault, Mater,' he protested, 'if I catch a cold in the head.'

His mother turned her eyes towards him and he wilted under the stare.

'Better have a cold than nothing!' she said curtly, and with a resigned shrug of his shoulders Eustace gave up the argument.

John was about to suggest that they might go back to the fire in the drawing room, for in spite of the central heating, the hall was chilly, when Peggy stiffened suddenly and looked towards the front door.

'Listen!' she said.

'What is it?' he asked.

'I thought I heard the sound of a car coming up the drive,' she answered.

They listened in silence and presently heard the faint hum of an engine and the soft swish of wheels on wet gravel.

'It must be Gore returning at last,' muttered John with an audible sigh of relief.

'There you are, you see,' cried Georgina triumphantly. 'I was right! You'll find that he's had a puncture or something — '

'It's stopped!' broke in Peggy.

The sound of the wheels and the soft hum of the engine had ceased suddenly. John uttered an impatient exclamation.

'What the devil has he stopped for halfway down the drive,' he grunted.

'Let's hope he's run over the gentleman in black,' sneered Georgina. 'That'll put an end to all the nonsense.'

'Except the footsteps and the noises in the night,' said Peggy quietly.

The elder woman lifted one shoulder

'You want a plumber to deal with those!' she answered contemptuously.

'I say, what was that?' said Eustace suddenly. 'Did you hear anything?'

His mother turned towards him angrily.

'Are you beginning to hear things now?' she said scornfully. 'Good God, it's catching!'

'I distinctly heard a sound like someone drumming with their knuckles on the door,' insisted her son stubbornly. 'Listen, there it is again!'

'I heard it that time,' said John. 'What is it?'

The sound came again, a soft swishing noise as though someone were scrabbling at the panels with their fingers. It was followed by a faint tap. Fordyce went over to the door and pulled back the catch. As he jerked it open a gust of wind blew in and rustled the draperies in the hall. He stared out into the darkness, but there was nobody there. The porch was deserted!

'That's funny,' he muttered, the door still half open in his hand. 'I could have sworn somebody knocked.'

'I'm sure they did,' declared Eustace, 'I heard it twice most distinctly!'

'Well, there's no one there,' said John, 'and they couldn't — Hello, here's something on the step!'

He stooped and picked up a square brown paper parcel.

'Good God, my books!' he exclaimed as he caught sight of the label. 'It must have been Gore who was knocking! I wonder why he didn't take them round to the back.'

'Oh, God!' cried Peggy suddenly, and pointed to the parcel he still held in his hand. 'Look there's *blood* on it!'

John stared down and the colour left his face. On the side of the parcel was a large irregular stain that glistened in the soft light from the hall lamp. He touched it with his finger, and the tip came away red and sticky. It was undoubtedly blood, and it was still fresh!

5

Murder!

John Fordyce looked up from the blood-stained parcel, and his face was set and grave.

'It looks as though Gore has met with an accident after all,' he said, and Wainwright nodded.

'Don't you think we'd better go outside and see if we can find him?' he suggested.

'The parcel couldn't have got on the step by itself, and it looks to me as though he just had strength enough to reach the door, and then collapsed.'

John nodded and setting down the parcel went over to his coat. The flashlamp was still in the pocket, where he had left it after their previous excursion, and from the open doorway he flashed its light on to the steps. There was a small patch of blood on the top one where the parcel had rested and several more leading down in an irregular trail to the gravel, but here they became lost in the wet. Wainwright had joined him by now, and together they went down the steps and made a quick search in the vicinity of the porch, but there was no sign of Gore, injured or otherwise. About halfway down the drive, however, they saw the dim lights of a motionless car.

'That must be my car,' said John, and set off towards it.

It was his car and they found that it was slewed round so that the front wheels were almost buried in the bushes on the right hand side of the drive. The engine was not running, and when Wainwright opened the door, and peered into the interior, he found that the car was empty.

'He's not here,' he said, and John's brows met in a puzzled frown.

'I don't understand it at all,' he muttered. 'What made him stop the car so far from the house?'

Without answering Wainwright took the torch from his hand, and turned its light on the wet ground.

'It looks as if he had pulled up to avoid

running into something,' he said after a moment's examination. 'Look at this churned up gravel by the back wheels.' He pointed to a ridge that the tyres had scooped up. 'He jammed on his brakes suddenly, and the car skidded. That accounts for its position.'

'But what happened to him after that?' said the bewildered John.

Wainwright shrugged his shoulders. He was still fanning the wet drive with the light of the torch, moving slowly back towards the house as he did so. A few yards from the front of the car he stopped.

'What do you make of this?' he said softly, and John looked down at a confusion of footprints that showed up clearly in the white circle of light.

'It looks to me as though there'd been a struggle of some description,' he said, frowning.

'It does to me,' replied his friend significantly, 'and here's a trail of prints that have broken away from this confused jumble and appear to lead towards the house.'

He began to follow them up and John saw to his surprise that apparently the person who had made them had been walking on tiptoe. He mentioned this to Wainwright, but the other shook his head impatiently.

'No, he was running,' he said curtly.

'Running?' echoed John. 'Why?'

'Away from the other man,' said Wainwright. 'There are two sets of prints here. I don't know which are Gore's, but at a guess I should say he was the man who was running away.'

The prints led up as far as the wide circular space in front of the house, but here the gravel was harder and they were more difficult to follow. They picked up a faint trace of them, however, near the lower step, and there they ended.

'Well, that's that,' said Wainwright biting his lips, and staring at the ground. 'Evidently Gore wasn't wounded in the car, or there would have been blood on the cushions. I should say that whatever happened to him happened just as he reached the front door.'

'But what could have happened to

him?' exclaimed John irritably. 'And where is he?'

Wainwright shook his head.

'Don't ask me,' he replied. 'He must have reached the porch to leave the parcel there.' He scratched his chin. 'There's no doubt he was seriously wounded. He must have lost a considerable amount of blood. The state of these steps and the parcel proves that. Perhaps, thinking he couldn't make anybody hear at the front, he tried to crawl round to the back. Let's try there.'

Accompanied by John, he walked round the entire house, flashing his light in every place that offered concealment for a wounded man. But they found nothing; Gore had apparently completely vanished.

They came back to the hall puzzled, worried and soaked to the skin.

'Well?' said Peggy eagerly.

'It's not at all well,' answered John shortly. 'There's no sign of Gore anywhere.'

The girl's eyes widened in amazement.

'No sign of him?' she repeated. 'But I

heard the car, or wasn't it our car?'

'It was our car all right,' said John grimly, 'but Gore wasn't in it.'

'He must have come in it,' said Peggy, wrinkling her forehead, 'or he couldn't have brought the parcel.'

'We've no proof that he did bring the parcel,' put in Wainwright, quietly.

They stared at him.

'Then how did it get on the steps?' Peggy demanded. 'Somebody brought it.'

'Somebody brought it,' he agreed nodding, 'but we've no proof that it was Gore.'

'Well, I don't see who else it could be,' argued John, and Wainwright smiled.

'Neither do I,' he admitted. 'I'm only pointing out that because Gore went away in your car, it doesn't necessarily follow that he came back in it.'

'Might I suggest,' broke in Georgina, who up till now had been sitting on the oak settee silently smoking, 'that most likely Gore is at the moment in the kitchen?'

They were so staggered at her words that for a moment they could only stare at her in silence.

'Why do you think that?' asked Peggy.

'Because,' she answered coolly, 'it seems to me that you're so busy all of you trying to make a mystery that you've overlooked the most obvious explanation.'

'What is your explanation, then, Mrs. Yapp?' said Wainwright with interest.

Georgina blew out a cloud of smoke and watched it drift towards the raftered ceiling.

'Simply that the man's nose was bleeding,' she replied surprisingly. 'It's quite possible that he had to stop the car halfway down the drive, brought John's books up to the front door, slipped on the wet steps, and banged his nose against the panel. That would account for the blood and that peculiar noise we heard, which was certainly nobody knocking in the ordinary way.'

'By Jove!' exclaimed Wainwright approvingly. 'That's a very ingenious suggestion, Mrs. Yapp.'

'Thank you,' retorted Georgina, 'there are times when I'm quite intelligent!'

'But what did Gore do after that?' said John by no means convinced.

'I suggest,' replied Georgina, 'that he walked round to the kitchen in order to attend to his nose.'

'Well, that's easily found out,' said John. Anne was just coming down the stairs and he called her: 'Anne, will you see if Gore is in the kitchen?'

She looked at him a little startled.

'Why, sir,' she said, 'has he come back then?'

'That's what I want to know,' said John.

She gave him a wondering look, but without saying anything disappeared through the door leading to the back of the house. In less than two minutes she had returned.

'He's not there, sir,' she said.

John shot a glance at Georgina, but she was smoking quietly and appeared to be taking not the slightest interest in what was going on.

'Could he have gone up to his room?' suggested Wainwright.

Anne shook her head.

'Not unless he came in the front way, sir,' she answered. 'Cook's been in the kitchen all the time, she would have seen him.'

'Well, that's that,' said John. 'The man can't be in the house at all.'

'It's very funny, you know,' remarked Eustace.

'Oh, very,' snapped Georgina looking round; 'we're all screaming with laughter!'

'I think we ought to do something,' said John in a worried voice. 'The man may be seriously hurt — '

He broke off as Anne gave a half stifled exclamation.

'Why do you say that, sir?' she asked. 'What's happened?' He told her and her face went white.

'I knew something would happen,' she cried wildly. 'When I heard about that man in the drive. He's at the bottom of it!'

She broke down, sobbing jerkily. 'Don't be stupid, girl!' said Georgina crossly; 'things are quite bad enough without you having hysterics.' With an effort the housemaid checked her tears. 'I'm sorry, ma'am,' she said quietly, and then looking at Fordyce: 'May I have the dirty glasses from the library, sir?'

He was so occupied with his own thoughts, that it is doubtful if he heard what she said, but he nodded mechanically, and she crossed over to the library door. Her scream a second later sent them all running white-faced to the threshold of the room. 'Anne, what's the matter?' cried John, as the girl came staggering out of the doorway, her hands before her face.

'Oh, my God!' she muttered brokenly. 'Look, in there — on the floor.'

She swayed and Wainwright was just in time to catch her as she fell. John took two steps forward into the library, and stopped dead, staring in horror at the thing he saw.

'What is it, Jack?' asked Peggy from the open doorway, and he waved her away.

'Don't come in,' he said sharply. 'Wainwright, don't let her come in here.'

Crumpled up by the french windows lay the figure of a man, and without looking at his face John recognised him by the neat uniform that he wore. It was Gore!

Going over he bent down. The carpet

under the man was stained with blood, and blood was still oozing from a narrow slit in the breast of the tunic. It only needed one glance to see that he was dead, for the sightless eyes were wide open and staring at the ceiling.

6

A Scrap of Paper

John withdrew his gaze from the horror of those staring eyes and went quickly back to the library door.

'Come here, Wainwright, will you,' he called huskily. 'And don't let any of the others come in.'

'What's happened?' It was Peggy who spoke.

'Something rather dreadful,' said John quickly.

He found it difficult to keep his voice under control, and her wide frightened eyes searched his enquiringly.

'Is it — is it Gore?' she whispered.

He nodded. It was useless trying to keep the truth from her, she would have to know sooner or later.

'Yes, and I'm afraid he's dead,' he answered.

Her face, pale before, went even paler.

'How — dreadful,' she murmured. 'How — how — ?' she left the sentence unfinished but John knew what she was trying to say.

'He has been stabbed, I think,' he said soberly. 'Will you come, Harry?'

Harry Wainwright, who was bending over the limp form of Anne, which he had placed in a chair, straightened up and nodded briefly.

'Yes,' he said, 'will one of you look after this girl?'

'I will,' said Georgina, and took his place beside the unconscious housemaid.

Wainwright followed John into the library and they closed the door.

'There he is, over there,' said John and pointed to the still form by the window. His hand was shaking badly.

'Pull yourself together,' said Wainwright. 'Have some of that.'

He nodded towards the whisky on the table, and John followed his advice. While he gulped down a generous portion of the spirit his friend went over and looked down into the upturned face of the dead man. John heard the hiss of his breath as he drew it in sharply.

'There's no doubt that he's dead,' he murmured, and stooping, peered more closely at the narrow slit in the tunic. 'Stabbed, too. You ought to telephone at once for a doctor.'

'And the police,' added John.

Wainwright nodded and straightened up.

'Yes, I'm afraid you'll have to notify them,' he said. 'This is obviously murder.'

'I'd better go and telephone now,' said John, and went out of the room.

When he had gone, Wainwright knelt down, beside the dead man, and without disturbing the position of the body, went rapidly through his pockets.

If he was looking for anything in particular he apparently did not find it, for presently he shook his head and rising to his feet turned his attention to the french windows. When Fordyce came back he was examining the fastenings.

'The police will be here almost directly,' said John, and his friend grunted and looked up.

'Did you know these windows were

69

unfastened?' he asked.

'No,' John went over to his side, 'they weren't the last time I was here.'

'That was just after I came, wasn't it?' asked Wainwright, and he nodded. 'Well, somebody must have come in and opened them after that.'

He pulled one of the windows open and looked down at the ground outside.

'There's blood on the sill, and on the step,' he went on. 'It looks to me as if the actual stabbing had taken place by the front door step, and that Gore afterwards staggered round here in a wounded condition. It's not so very far.'

'He couldn't have known the windows were open?' broke in John.

'I don't think he did,' replied Wainwright shaking his head. 'Look here,' he pointed to a long smear on the glass outside, 'that's the mark of a hand,' he said, 'and here, on the lower part of the door is a smudged blood stain. What I think happened was this. He got as far as the windows when death overtook him, and fell against them. They were unfastened and opened under his touch and he fell into the room.

Probably he wasn't quite dead when that happened, and managed to crawl a few inches farther before his strength gave out.'

'That sounds possible,' muttered John, 'but who opened the windows in the first place?'

'I'd rather like to know that myself,' said Wainwright softly. He came over to the centre of the room, and stood rubbing his chin thoughtfully.

'What do you know about this man, Gore?' he remarked after a pause.

'I don't know anything about him except that he was a very good chauffeur,' answered John. 'Anne recommended him, and his references were excellent.'

'Oh, Anne recommended him, did she?' interrupted Wainwright looking up sharply. 'Then she knew him?'

'Yes,' said John. 'She told me they'd been in service together before.'

'Perhaps she'll be able to tell us something more when she recovers,' said his friend. He gave a quick glance round the room. 'In the meanwhile there's nothing we can do until the police come, so we may as well get out of here. It's not very pleasant.'

John agreed with him in this, and when they had left the room of death with its silent occupant, and locked the door behind them, he felt relieved. The shock of the discovery had left him white and shaken, and he wanted to recover before the ordeal of the police investigations. They found Peggy and Georgina in the drawing room huddled round the remains of the dying fire, and learned that Anne had recovered and had gone to her room in charge of Mrs. Docker. The rest of the servants had been told of the tragedy, and while they were talking, Nellie, her eyes swollen with crying, and her face twitching and frightened, came in with fresh coal to make up the fire.

'Ask Cook to make some coffee, Nellie,' said Peggy, as the girl fumbled nervously with the coal.

'Yes, miss,' muttered Nellie.

Her hands were trembling so violently that she dropped the tongs she was using, and they fell with a clatter in the fender. Such was the state of their nerves that the noise made them all jump. She apologised incoherently, and ran out of the room like a frightened rabbit.

'What's happened to Eustace?' asked John looking round for that flamboyant youth.

'I've sent him to bed,' answered Georgina. 'He was fussing about and becoming a nuisance.'

'I'm afraid he'll have to get up again when the police arrive,' remarked Wainwright. 'They will want to see him.'

She looked at him coldly. 'Then they'll have to want,' she retorted. 'I've sent him to bed and there he'll stay! Anyhow, he knows nothing about this business, so he can't help them.'

'They'll want to decide that,' said Wainwright shrugging his shoulders; but she did not answer.

They had a long wait before the whirr of wheels heralded the arrival of the police, and they spent the time for the most part in silence, occupied by their own gloomy thoughts. Inspector Jukes when he did arrive looked a little dishevelled. He had, as he explained later,

73

been in bed when the news arrived, and they had had to send round from the police station to awaken him.

He had brought with him a sergeant and two uniformed policemen, and a little man in plain clothes, whom he introduced to John as Doctor Parker, the police surgeon. He listened, frowning portentously, while John told him what had happened.

'I'd like to see the body first, sir,' he said, when he had heard the circumstances of the crime, 'and after that I shall want to see everybody in the house.'

In silence John led the way across the hall, and unlocked the library door. The inspector paused on the threshold, and gazed round the room, his little eyes narrowed until they were almost completely closed, then he walked over to the window and looked down at the dead man.

'H'm! This is a bad business,' he remarked, shaking his head. 'Will you get on with your examination, Doctor?'

Doctor Parker, who had evidently been waiting rather impatiently to do this, gave a quick affirmative jerk to his rather narrow head, and knelt down beside the body. He was less than two minutes making his examination, then he looked up.

'The man was stabbed with a narrow bladed knife,' he said fixing his glasses more firmly on the bridge of his rather thin nose. 'The wound appears to have missed the heart, but has severed one of the larger blood vessels. He's practically bled to death.'

'Then he didn't die at once?' said Jukes.

'No, no.' Doctor Parker rose to his feet and brushed the knees of his trousers. 'Death must have followed some little time after he was stabbed. There'll have to be an autopsy, of course; I can tell you more after that.'

'Thanks, Doctor,' said Jukes. 'I'll just run through the pockets and we'll take a couple of photographs, and then we can get this fellow away on the ambulance.'

He stooped over the dead man and searched his clothing. The contents of the pockets were not numerous, and these he piled in a little heap on the floor. There was a small amount of money; a rather worn pocketbook; a bunch of keys; a watch, and a large clasp knife. The inspector, slightly red of face from his exertion, looked at this meagre collection and grunted.

'Not much there,' he remarked, 'unless there's anything in the pocketbook.'

He picked it up, and peered into the various compartments. Apparently he found nothing of interest, for presently he put it back with the other things, and called to one of the two policemen.

'All right, Trender,' he said. 'You can get busy now. Two photographs will be enough. One showing the position of the body, and a close-up.'

Trender, who had been carrying a small black case, came forward, and began to unpack a camera. He set this up on a folding tripod, and proceeded to prepare a flashlight apparatus.

'We're lucky having Trender, sir,' explained Inspector Jukes. 'His hobby's photography, and it saves us a lot of trouble in a case like this.'

He waited until the photographs had been taken, and then issued his instructions for the removal of the body.

'You won't want me any more, will you?' asked Doctor Parker, as all that remained of the unfortunate chauffeur was carried out, and Jukes shook his head.

'No, Doctor,' he said. 'You'll let me have your report at the station?'

The police surgeon nodded.

'First thing in the morning,' he replied, and with a jerk of the head to John and Wainwright, went out in the wake of the two policemen who were carrying the body.

'Now, sir,' said Inspector Jukes, coughing as the acrid smoke from the flashlight powder irritated his throat. 'You say it was your housemaid who first made the discovery? I'd like to see her.'

John looked a little doubtful.

'She was very much upset by the shock,' he said, 'and she hasn't had much time to recover. Couldn't you question her later?'

The inspector caressed his large chin and frowned.

'Well I don't know, sir — ' he began,

and noticing his hesitation, Wainwright hastened to add:

'I don't think she can tell you much, Inspector. She wasn't in here more than a second before she screamed.'

'Well,' said Jukes, 'if it'll give her a chance to pull herself together, I'll make my investigations outside first. But I shall have to see her. Perhaps you'll tell her that, sir?'

He walked heavily over to the french windows.

'You say these were open?' he said peering at the hasp. 'Do you know who opened them?'

John shook his head.

'No, we were puzzling over that,' he answered. 'Mr. Wainwright and I were in there earlier in the evening and the windows were fastened then.'

'H'm,' said the Inspector. 'Well, sir, somebody must have come in and opened them after that. They haven't been tampered with.'

He scratched his head gently.

'The thing is, was this fellow killed in here or outside?'

'I don't see how he could have been killed in here,' said Wainwright, and gave his reasons.

Inspector Jukes listened attentively, nodding every now and again in agreement.

'Your idea seems feasible, sir,' he commented. 'I think I'll have a look round outside.'

He opened the windows and paused on the threshold.

'You won't forget to call your housemaid so that I can see her when I come back, sir?' he said looking at John. 'I don't want to waste more time than I can help.'

There was a subtle note of reproach in his voice, and John took the hint.

'I'll go and warn her now,' he said, and left the room.

Inspector Jukes went outside and looked about him. The rain had stopped but the night was still cloudy, and very dark. Taking an electric torch from his pocket he swept the light over the step and the path beyond. Wainwright pointed out the blood mark on the lower part of the window, and the hand smear on the glass.

'It seems to bear out your theory, sir,' said Jukes. 'The trouble is the rain will have washed away any traces there might have been on the path.'

He looked round as he heard the library door open and close, and called to one of the policemen who had just come in.

'Here, Corbett,' he said, 'go down and stay by that car in the drive, and don't let anybody touch it. I shall want to look at that in a minute.'

'Which car, sir?' asked the constable stupidly.

'The first one, you fool!' snapped his superior. 'The one we couldn't pass when we arrived.'

The policeman looked a little aggrieved.

'You might have meant the one by the front door, sir,' he said in an injured voice.

'I might have meant the one in the garage at Tor Bridge, but I didn't,' growled Jukes. 'Where's Trender?'

'On guard in the hall, sir,' answered the constable.

'Right, tell him to stop there,' said the

inspector, and the man departed to carry out his orders.

Jukes returned to his examination of the path outside the french windows, but except for the blood mark on the narrow step, there were no other traces of Gore's progress. If the man had crawled round from the front porch in a wounded condition, which seemed the only sensible explanation, the heavy rain had washed away all signs he may have left.

Jukes was conscientious, however, if a little slow, and he followed the narrow path, searching it patiently.

It was Wainwright who made the only discovery worthwhile and this was a staggering one.

He was walking by the side of Jukes, and they had almost reached the drawing room windows when something white in the middle of a clump of evergreens, attracted his attention. He went over, and found that it was a scrap of paper, wedged in the fork of a branch. Reaching out he detached it from its resting place, and looked at it. It was crumpled and dirty, and had apparently been torn out of a notebook. In the dim light from the window behind him, he was able to make out some scrawled words in pencil. He called to Jukes to bring his lamp, and the inspector came over to his side.

'What is it, sir?' he asked curiously.

'I don't know,' said Wainwright, 'it may be nothing. Put your light on it, will you?'

The inspector shone the ray of his torch on the oblong paper, and with difficulty Wainwright made out the hastily written message. His brows drew together as he did so, and he whistled softly.

'What do you make of that?' he said, and held the sodden sheet of paper so that Jukes could read it for himself.

'*You don't realize your peril, but you will! This house is dangerous for you and yours. Leave it!*'

There was no signature.

7

Inspector Jukes Takes Charge

'That message explains the stone through the window,' said Wainwright.

Inspector Jukes nodded ponderously. He was seated at one end of the long refectory table in the dining room, a notebook open by his side, and before him the crumpled sheet of paper that Wainwright had found in the bushes.

'Yes, sir, I think you're right,' he said thoughtfully. 'This message was wrapped round the stone, and fell off after the person, whoever it was, had thrown it.'

He looked across at John Fordyce who was standing in front of the recently lit fire.

'Now, sir,' he said, 'before I go any further I'd like to ask you a few questions.'

'Carry on, Inspector,' said John. 'I'll tell you anything I can.'

Jukes consulted his notebook frowningly, and there was a short silence before he spoke again.

'About a week ago, sir,' he proceeded at length, 'to be exact, on the seventh of the month, you rang up the police station and laid information regarding an attempt that had been made to break into this house?'

'Quite right,' said John. 'I did.'

'On the same occasion,' continued Jukes, 'you told me that several times a man dressed in black and wearing a muffler over his face had been seen by yourself and the servants lurking about in the vicinity of the house, and you believed that it was this prowler who had attempted the burglary?'

'Quite correct, Inspector.'

'Now, sir,' said Jukes turning over a leaf of his notebook, 'I understand that this man was seen again tonight?'

'Last night,' interrupted Wainwright gently; 'it's after twelve Inspector.'

Jukes looked up at him angrily.

'I'll trouble you not to interrupt me, sir,' he said stiffly.

Wainwright shrugged his shoulders.

'I only thought it was just as well to be accurate,' he remarked. 'Sorry.'

Jukes repeated his question, and John nodded.

'I believe he was,' he said.

The inspector raised his eyebrows.

'You only believe he was,' he said, 'you didn't see him yourself then?'

'No,' answered John.

'I see,' Jukes rubbed gently at his chin. 'Now have you any reason to suppose that this man had anything to do with the murder of your chauffeur?'

'My dear Inspector,' protested John. 'How can I possibly answer a question like that?'

The inspector's small eyes regarded him suspiciously.

'Does that mean,' he said slowly, 'that you refuse to answer the question?'

John made a gesture of annoyance.

'Certainly not!' he answered. 'It means I can't answer it. I know nothing about the man or why Gore should have been killed.'

Jukes accepted this explanation in

silence, but from the expression on his face he was obviously not satisfied.

'At the time Gore met his death,' he went on after a moment's pause, 'he was, I believe, returning from an errand on which you had sent him?'

'Yes,' agreed John, 'he had gone over to Tor Bridge to collect a parcel of books that were waiting for me at the station.'

'And he was late in returning?'

'Very late,' said John, 'in fact we all wondered what could have happened to him.'

'How long had he been in your employ?' asked the inspector.

'Just over three weeks.' John was getting a little impatient. All this ground had been covered before. He could see no reason why they should go over it again. But Inspector Jukes apparently thought otherwise.

'Are you aware of anything concerning Gore's private life that might suggest a motive for his murder?' he continued.

John shook his head irritably.

'No, if I was, I should have told you,' he said.

The inspector's brows contracted, and he picked up the soiled paper in front of him.

'Do you attach any importance to this message?' he asked.

'I know no more about it than you do,' replied John.

'H'm!' Jukes laid it down and leaned back in his chair. 'This is a very puzzling case, sir. A very puzzling case indeed. So far nobody seems to know anything.'

Wainwright smiled dryly.

'Most inconsiderate of them, Inspector,' he remarked.

The inspector shot him a quick glance, and opened his lips as though he were about to make some retort, but instead he turned to John.

'There's nothing more then, sir,' he said, 'that you can tell me?'

'No, I'm afraid I've told you all I know,' answered John politely.

'Then I'd like to see the lady who is staying with you,' Jukes glanced at his notebook. 'Mrs. Yapp.'

'I'll fetch her,' offered Wainwright obligingly, and crossed over to the door.

While he was waiting for the arrival of Georgina, Jukes consulted his notes, and made a few further entries, with a gravity that nearly made John disgrace himself by laughing.

Georgina came in smoking the inevitable cigarette, and surveyed Jukes through her monocle as though he were some extraordinary object that she was viewing at an exhibition.

'You wanted to speak to me?' she asked.

He nodded and gave a preliminary cough.

'I should like you to tell me, Madam,' he said, 'in your own words, exactly what led up to the discovery of this crime.'

She told him briefly and concisely.

'It was your son, I believe, Madam,' he said when she had finished, 'who first heard the noise at the front door that led to Mr. Fordyce discovering the parcel on the step?'

'It was,' answered Georgina curtly. 'He's always doing something damned silly!'

Jukes looked a little shocked, but he went on without comment.

'I should like to put some questions to him. Can I see him?'

She shrugged her shoulders.

'Certainly, if you think you can withstand the shock,' she said.

Her answer rather staggered him.

'What do you mean by that, Madam?' he said a little puzzled.

'At the present moment he is in bed,' she answered coolly.

'Oh, I see,' he drew a long breath, and his sallow face flushed.

'I don't wish to jump to conclusions,' he said sternly, 'but I hope that you aren't by any chance trying to be funny at a time like this?'

She met his gaze with an expressionless face.

'The mere thought of attempting anything humorous in your presence appals me Inspector!' she said seriously.

'I'm glad of that, Madam,' answered Jukes with dignity. 'Now if you please, will you go and wake your son, and tell him I wish to speak to him?'

'Certainly not!' she answered.

He stared at her, with his mouth half open.

'What did you say, Madam?' he asked.

'I said, certainly not!' repeated Georgina coolly. 'He's much better off where he is!'

The inspector gasped like a newly landed fish, and for a moment Wainwright feared that he was going to lose his temper, but by an effort he managed to control himself.

'I'm afraid, Madam, you don't realise the gravity of the situation,' he said patiently. 'A serious crime has been committed and I — er — representing the law am trying to collect evidence regarding it with the intention of bringing to justice the person or persons responsible.'

This rather bombastic speech had no effect on Georgina at all.

'It's nice of you to explain what you're doing,' she said sweetly, and John seeing the veins in Jukes' neck swell dangerously, thought it was time to interfere.

'I think you'd better fetch Eustace down,' he said. 'The inspector's quite right, and he's only doing his duty.'

'Very well,' she said, 'but I warn you, he's only going to be a nuisance.'

She sailed majestically out of the room, and presently Eustace entered. He was dressed in a vividly coloured dressing gown, and mauve silk pyjamas, and had obviously paused to carefully brush his hair. He blinked round at them a little sleepily, and yawned.

'Isn't all this too divinely exciting?' he remarked. 'I'm so glad Mater wakened me.'

'I'm sorry to have disturbed you, sir — ' began Jukes, but without taking the slightest notice of him Eustace went on:

'One comes to welcome anything that breaks the monotony of life. Life's so dull, don't you think?'

'I should like, sir — ' said Jukes in a louder voice.

'Do you know I've got an idea for such a charming little sonnet,' continued Eustace blithely. 'The inspiration came to me while I was brushing my hair. It's extraordinary the times these thoughts enter my mind.'

'I really must ask you to attend to me, sir!' roared Jukes, very red in the face.

Eustace looked at him in mild surprise.

'Are you speaking to me?' he said. 'I'm so sorry. What is it?'

'I want to ask you some questions,' said the inspector loudly, and Eustace held up his hand with a pained expression.

'Please — ' he said, screwing up his face, 'would you mind lowering your voice? It's so harsh, and anything approaching discord is abhorrent to my sensitive ear.'

'Oh,' Jukes blinked at him, and went on in a lower tone. 'Well then, sir, I want — '

'That's much better!' said Eustace encouragingly. 'Perhaps a *little* more piano, if you could manage it, would be an improvement.'

For a moment it seemed there was danger that the inspector might have a fit.

'Don't keep interrupting me!' he snapped in a voice hoarse with anger. 'Now regarding what happened last night — '

Eustace gave a little squeal of dismay.

'Oh, really, I can't let you talk about that!' he said. 'In my present mood I couldn't bear to listen to anything horrid!'

Jukes looked helplessly at John and Wainwright.

'You see,' explained Eustace, 'my mind is full of spring, and flowers and birds at the moment. Couldn't you talk to me some other time?'

'No, sir!' roared Jukes explosively, 'I could not!'

Eustace looked at him pathetically.

'That's very tiresome of you,' he said.

'You must answer Inspector Jukes' questions,' said John, and he gave a sigh of resignation.

'Oh, well if I must, I must,' he said. 'Go on, Inspector.'

'I believe you were the first person,' said Jukes, 'who heard the tapping on the front door?'

'Yes,' answered Eustace. 'The thought of it makes me shiver.'

'Will you confine yourself to answering my questions,' snapped Jukes. 'Now after you heard this noise the second time, Mr. Fordyce opened the front door and discovered the bloody parcel?'

'If you're going to use such shocking language,' interrupted Eustace, 'I shan't listen to you any more, Inspector. I shan't really.'

'I'm merely describing the state of the parcel,' grunted the harassed Jukes.

'Well, you could easily have said sanguinary,' protested Eustace. 'It would have been so much more delicate!'

The inspector swallowed hard, and his flushed face went purple.

'I warn you, sir,' he said angrily, 'that I am getting to the end of my patience. Will you kindly stop these interruptions and tell me what you know?'

'I know nothing,' answered Eustace. 'Nothing at all! I just heard a noise at the front door, and that was all I had to do with it.'

Jukes put several more questions, but Eustace could supply him with no further information, and eventually, to his obvious relief, he dismissed him.

When the youth had gone, the inspector wiped his perspiring face with a large handkerchief and looked across at John.

'Now, sir,' he said, 'if you think your housemaid has quite recovered, I should like to hear what *she* has to say.'

8

Death in the Drive

When Anne came in a little later there were few visible traces of her recent terror. Her face was rather paler than usual, but otherwise she was quite composed.

'You sent for me, sir?' she said addressing John.

He nodded.

'Yes,' he answered. 'Inspector Jukes would like to ask you a few questions.'

She turned her head towards the bulky figure of the inspector seated at the end of the long table, and waited in silence.

Jukes cleared his throat, and turned over the pages of his notebook before he began.

'Your name is Anne Barton?' he said at last, and it was more of a statement than a question.

'Yes, sir,' answered the housemaid. Her

voice was low and toneless, and the only outward sign of emotion she showed, was in the hand that gripped the edge of the table by which she was standing.

'I understand,' went on the inspector, 'that you were previously acquainted with this man, Gore?'

'Yes, sir,' she said again. 'I met him when I was at Mrs. Mirthwaite's.'

'How long ago was that?' said Jukes.

She was thoughtful for a moment before she replied.

'Nearly two years,' she said after a pause.

'Were you in service at — Mrs. — ' he boggled over the name, and she repeated it quietly.

'Mrs. Mirthwaite's? — yes, sir.'

'And was Gore the chauffeur there?' he asked.

She nodded.

'Did you know him very well?' Jukes continued.

'Not very well,' she answered shaking her head. 'Not more than any of the other servants.'

'Can you tell us anything,' said Jukes,

'that is likely to help us in finding a motive for his death?'

Her eyes flickered, and the hand gripping the end of the table tightened its grasp until the knuckles stood out white.

'Nothing,' she said shortly.

There was a perceptible pause before the inspector put his next question.

'Why did you recommend him to Mr. Fordyce?' he asked.

'Mr. Fordyce mentioned one day that he was looking for a chauffeur, sir,' she replied, 'and I knew that Gore was a very good chauffeur, and that he was out of work.'

'You knew his address, then?' said Jukes quickly.

For the fraction of a second she was a little disconcerted.

'Yes, sir,' she answered, 'he had just left Mrs. Mirthwaite's, and he knew I was going to this new job, and asked me if I heard of anything to let him know.'

'Why did he leave Mrs. Mirthwaite's?' said the inspector.

'They were giving up the car, sir,' she answered. 'Mr. Mirthwaite lost a lot of money in the depression.'

'Is that why you left?' asked Jukes.

She nodded. The inspector frowned, and jotted down a note in his book.

'What was this address he gave you?' he continued presently.

Again she hesitated.

'29a Fairlawn Road, Exeter,' she said and Jukes raised his eyebrows.

'Exeter?' he exclaimed, and she added quickly:

'He wanted to get a job outside London. He preferred the country. Mr. and Mrs. Mirthwaite lived in Grosvenor Square.'

The inspector looked by no means satisfied with this explanation, but he did not pursue the subject.

'Did Gore say anything to you or any of the other servants before he went to Tor Bridge on this errand for Mr. Fordyce?' he asked.

'I don't quite know what you mean, sir,' she answered.

'Well,' said Jukes, 'was he nervous at all did he say that he might be a long time — '

'Oh no, sir,' she broke in hastily.

Jukes' small eyes searched her face.

'Why,' he said slowly, 'were you frightened when he didn't come back as soon as he should have done?'

'I'd heard all about this man in the drive,' she answered returning his gaze steadily, 'and — well, I was afraid something might have happened.'

'You connected this man in the drive with Gore?' he asked.

'No, sir,' she replied. 'But I knew he was there again last night. Cook saw him, and I was just — scared.'

'H'm,' said Jukes. He dropped his eyes to his notebook, and gazed at it for a moment or two in silence,

'You complained to Mr. Fordyce last night,' he said suddenly, 'about some noises you'd heard in the house. What were they, and when did you hear them?'

Anne told him, in practically the same words that she had used to John previously. Jukes listened without comment, but when she had finished he asked:

'Do you associate these noises with the

man in the drive?'

She shook her head.

'I don't associate them with anything, sir,' she said quietly. 'I only think that it's all very strange.'

'You've never seen this man yourself?' said the inspector, and again she shook her head.

'No, sir,' she answered.

He let her go, and turned to John.

'I'm not altogether satisfied with your housemaid,' he said. 'I've got an idea she's keeping something back.'

'I don't see why she should,' replied John. 'I think you're wrong, Inspector; I don't think she knows anything.'

'She seems to have known quite a lot about Gore,' grunted Jukes. 'Quite a lot that she hasn't told, too. I shall want to talk to her again later. In the meantime, I think I'd better see the rest of the servants.'

He gained very little information from them, however. Nellie was voluble over her experience with the masked man in the drive, and confirmed Anne's statement regarding the noises in the night.

She, herself, had heard them on several occasions. They were like someone shuffling about the house in slippers, and occasionally there were faint rappings. To use her own expression: 'like somebody tappin' on wood with a toffee 'ammer.'

Mrs. Docker, the stout cook, was less sensational. She had heard the noises too, but she was inclined to offer a practical explanation. Raven House was very old, and the sounds might be accounted for by the creaking of the ancient woodwork, or rats in the skirting, or lots of things. She had been in an old house before, and she had heard water in the pipes make funny sounds very similar to these they were discussing. She had certainly seen the man in the drive, and her description coincided with Nellie's. She knew nothing whatever about Gore, except that he was a nice quiet, respectable sort of fellow and she had liked him.

Jukes ended his long examination at last; dismissed Mrs. Docker, and rose rather wearily to his feet.

'I'll go down and examine that car now, sir,' he said closing his notebook and

101

stuffing it into the inside pocket of his tunic, 'and then I think I'll be getting back to the station.'

Trender was dozing in the hall when he came out of the dining room, but he jumped to his feet as Jukes approached him.

'You'd better come along with me,' said the inspector gruffly. 'I'll send Corbett up to take your place here.'

The sky was lightening in the east, and the chill of dawn was in the air as they walked down the semi-darkness of the drive. Corbett was standing by the motionless car, and Jukes sent him back to the house, with instructions to remain there, and see that nobody left.

With the aid of his lamp he made a careful examination of both the interior and the exterior of the car, but he found nothing, and presently he returned to the house to take his leave of John.

'I can do very little more here until the morning, sir,' he said. 'I shall be coming back then.'

John nodded. He was feeling very tired, and rather welcomed the prospect of getting rid of Jukes for a few hours. He offered the inspector a drink, which Jukes gladly accepted, and when he had swallowed it, he took his departure.

After the front door had closed behind him, John and Wainwright made their way to the drawing room, where they found Peggy all by herself, half asleep in a deep chair in front of the fire. She looked up with a start when they entered, and was surprised when John told her that the inspector had gone.

'Didn't he want to see me?' she demanded.

'Apparently not,' answered John. 'He never mentioned it, and I didn't remind him.'

'He's coming back in the morning,' remarked Wainwright, 'and he'll probably want to see you then. I should imagine that this was his first murder case, and that he was feeling the strain of the responsibility.'

She yawned.

'It's my first murder case, too,' she replied, 'and I think it's horrible. What's been happening?'

'Not much,' said John, 'except a whole string of questions, which I don't think have led or are likely to lead anywhere.'

He looked at her a little anxiously.

'Don't you think you'd better go to bed?' he added.

'I suppose I had,' she answered with a grimace. 'Eustace and Georgina went an hour ago. Georgina said she wasn't going to allow any murder to spoil her beauty sleep.'

'Did Eustace say the same?' asked Wainwright, his eyes twinkling, and she smiled.

'He didn't say it,' she replied. 'But I think he thought it!'

She wished them good night, and left them. When they were alone John looked at his friend.

'What are you going to do?' he asked. 'Are you going to get some sleep?'

Wainwright wrinkled his nose, and shook his head.

'No,' he answered. 'I never felt less like sleeping in my life. I shall sit here and smoke, I think. But you'd better get some rest.'

He eyed John critically.

'You look all in, and I expect you've got a heavy day before you.'

'I think I'll go and lie down anyway,' said John.

He crossed to the door.

'See you at breakfast, then.'

'You most certainly will,' answered Wainwright, 'and I wish it wasn't so far away!'

When John had gone, he poked the fire into a blaze, and making himself comfortable in an armchair, filled and lit his pipe. For a long time he smoked thoughtfully, and the dawn was well advanced when he got up, knocked the ashes out of his pipe, and went out into the hall. Corbett, seated by the front door, looked at him in surprise.

'Not gone to bed, sir?' he asked.

Wainwright shook his head.

'No,' he answered. 'Look here, constable, I want to get a breath of fresh air. Have you any objection if I take a stroll round the house?'

The policeman pursed his lips doubtfully.

105

'Well, sir,' he said, 'I've instructions to see that nobody leaves, but if you don't go no further than the gate, I suppose it'll be all right.'

Wainwright promised that he would keep within the confines of the grounds, and pulling on his overcoat opened the front door and passed out into the grey light of the morning. The air smelt cold and sweet, and after pausing for a moment at the foot of the steps, he began to walk slowly down the drive, sniffing appreciatively at its freshness . . .

John was sleeping soundly, when a hand shaking him by the shoulder roused him to wakefulness, and he sat up blinking a little resentfully at Wainwright, who was bending over him.

'What's the matter?' he asked, his voice husky with sleep.

'Something rather serious,' said his friend gravely. 'Get up, and come with me. There's been another murder! I have just found a dead man at the end of the drive!'

9

The Man From the Yard

John flung back the eiderdown, and swung his legs off the bed on to the floor. With the exception of his collar and tie he was still fully dressed, and sitting there he stared at Wainwright, still a little muzzy with sleep.

'What are you talking about?' he demanded rubbing his eyes.

'Wake up and pull yourself together!' said his friend sharply. 'I tell you there's been another murder. I've just found the body. In the bushes by the drive gates.'

John looked startled.

'Who is it?' he asked.

Wainwright shook his head.

'I don't know,' he replied. 'He's a stranger to me. That's why I came up and wakened you. I thought perhaps you might be able to recognise him.'

John was by this time more in

possession of his normal senses, and stooping he pulled on his shoes.

'I haven't told the constable yet,' said Wainwright as they left the bedroom together and walked towards the head of the stairs, 'so we'd better slip out the back way.'

John nodded and they passed down the big staircase in silence. Police-Constable Corbett looked at them rather curiously as they made their way towards the kitchen, but he said nothing, probably concluding that they were going to make themselves some tea.

The back door was bolted and chained, but they slipped the chain and drew back the bolts as quietly as possible, and opening the door, went out, closing it gently behind them. Making their way round the house by the little path that led into the drive, they hurried past the motionless car, and presently found themselves at the gates that gave on to the road. A few yards from these Wainwright stopped, and pointed to an irregular patch that stained the wet gravel.

'This is where he was killed,' he said in

a low voice, 'and the body was afterwards dragged over to the middle of these bushes.'

He went over to a thickly growing clump of evergreens, and gently parted the branches. Looking over his shoulder John saw the sprawling figure of a big man lying face upwards in the middle of them. He was dressed in a rather shabby blue serge suit and a heavy overcoat, which was unbuttoned and pulled open.

'Do you know him?' asked Wainwright, and John, staring at the heavy face, shook his head.

'Never seen him before in my life,' he declared. 'How was he killed?'

'He was stabbed the same way as Gore,' answered his friend. 'But for this bloodstain on the gravel, I should never have found him at all. I came out for a breath of fresh air and walked down as far as the gate, and then I saw this.'

He nodded at the dark patch.

'I saw that something had been dragged over the grass border, and following the track I came upon this fellow.'

John was still staring down at the body,

his face rather white.

'There must be a lunatic loose,' he muttered. 'I wonder when this man was killed?'

'Round about the same time as Gore, I should imagine,' answered Wainwright. 'The blood on his clothes has dried stiff.'

He let the crimson splashed branches that he had been holding back fall gently into place.

'We'd better go and tell the constable now,' he said, and John smothered a groan.

'That means that Jukes will come back and start all this questioning over again,' he grunted.

Wainwright shrugged his shoulders.

'I'm afraid he will,' he remarked, 'but it can't be helped.'

They went back to the house, and were admitted by the astonished Corbett. Before the constable, however, could put into words the question that was hovering on his lips, Wainwright had told him of his discovery. The man listened in horrified amazement.

'What, another?' he exclaimed. 'Do you

know who the man is, sir?'

Wainwright shook his head.

'No, I've told you all we know,' he answered. 'I think you'd better get on to the police station at once, and inform Inspector Jukes of this fresh development.'

The constable, who rather shirked the responsibility of dealing with this new murder on his own, agreed with alacrity and hurried away to the telephone.

They waited in silence for Corbett to come back. John was too staggered by the discovery of this second crime to talk, and Wainwright appeared to be completely occupied with his own thoughts.

When the constable did return he demanded to be taken at once to the place where the body had been found. On the way down the drive he told them that Jukes was leaving Tor Bridge immediately.

'This is the first time we've 'ad anythin' like this 'appen round 'ere,' he confided, 'most of our work is in runnin' in tramps and chicken thieves. But this looks like bein' a big case. I shouldn't be surprised if the Chief Constable didn't call in the Yard, though 'e won't if the Inspector can 'elp it,' he added with a grin. 'Is this the place, sir?' he went on as Wainwright stopped and the latter nodded and pointed to the bloodstain on the ground.

'That's where I think he was killed,' he said. 'The body is over there.'

He led the way over to the bushes, and Corbett stood looking down at the dead man and scratching his chin. He was a man above medium height; big-boned and fleshy. His face was large and heavy-jowled; the hair on his head sparse and flecked with grey. Wainwright judged his age to have been in the region of forty-five, and discovered later that he was only one year out in his reckoning.

The front of the man's waistcoat was soaked in blood, and in the middle of the stain was a narrow slit, which corresponded to the one they had seen in Gore's tunic. A few yards away from the body lay the dead man's hat. It was a bowler hat and the crown was dented and the brim broken as though it had been trodden on.

' 'E's a stranger in these parts,' remarked Corbett, after a moment's silence. 'But we may be able to find out who 'e is when we've searched the body.'

'Are you going to do that now?' asked John.

The constable shook his head.

'No, sir,' he answered. 'The inspector said as 'ow I wasn't to touch nothin' till 'e came.'

Wainwright, who had left them and had been peering about on his own, rejoined them with some fresh information.

'There was obviously some sort of a struggle,' he said. 'Near that stain on the ground the gravel is all churned up, and there's a confusion of footprints.'

'I don't think there's much doubt,' said Corbett heavily, 'that this feller was killed by the same man what killed the shuvver.'

'I don't think there's any doubt,' retorted Wainwright, shortly. 'I should say that what happened was this. After killing Gore the murderer was making his escape down the drive when he ran into this man, who either recognised him, or whom he was afraid would be able to identify him again. After a brief struggle, he stabbed him and dragged the body into these bushes and made his escape.'

'It's strange we didn't hear anything,' muttered John.

'I don't know,' said Wainwright, 'this is a good way from the house, and it's doubtful if the dead man had time to call for help.'

Corbett nodded slowly.

'That's most likely what 'appened, sir,' he agreed. 'It's a funny business altogether.'

'It doesn't make me laugh,' said John a little crossly. 'If I'd known this was going to happen, I'd never have come within miles of the place.'

'Perhaps it wouldn't have happened then,' remarked Wainwright. 'I wonder how long Jukes is going to be.'

''E said 'e was leaving at once, sir,' said the constable. 'So I shouldn't think 'e'd be very long. 'Is instructions was that I was to wait by the body until 'e arrived.'

It was a quarter of an hour later that they heard the chugging of the car engine that heralded the appearance of the inspector. His dilapidated little two-seater pulled up with a jerk outside the gate, and almost before it had stopped the bulky form of Jukes had precipitated itself from behind the wheel, and he hurried towards them. 'What's all this?' he greeted them breathlessly. 'Corbett tells me there's been another murder.'

'Corbett's right,' said John. 'There's the victim.'

Jukes pushed his way through the bushes and glared at the dead man.

'H'm,' he said. 'We'd better not move him until after the doctor's seen him. He'll be here directly. He was out on a case when I left, and I couldn't wait for him.'

He began to question them minutely, and was in the midst of this when a second car arrived and Doctor Parker joined them.

'Somebody's been working overtime here, haven't they?' growled the police surgeon when he was shown the body. 'H'm, stabbed the same as the other one.'

He unbuttoned the waistcoat and laid bare the wound.

'The same weapon was used too, I should imagine,' he went on. 'Looks as if the knife had passed clean through the heart, in which case he would have died instantaneously. I can tell you more definitely when I get him to the mortuary. Who is he?'

'We don't know yet,' said Jukes. 'When you've finished I'll go through his pockets, and see if there's anything by which he can be identified.'

'I've finished now,' said Parker rising to his feet. 'Carry on.'

The inspector stooped over the dead man, and began to run through his pockets. The overcoat yielded nothing, but in the inside breast pocket of the jacket he found a bulky wallet. This he opened and glanced through the contents. His exclamation, as he stared at a card that he had brought to light, caused four pairs of eyes to look at him enquiringly.

'Good God!' he said. 'This man was a police officer!'

'What was his name?' asked Wainwright, and the inspector looked at the card again.

'His name,' he said, 'was Blackwood, and he was a Detective-Inspector from Scotland Yard!'

10

Elford Arrives

Breakfast was nearly an hour late that morning. In the excitement of the night, Nellie, who was usually the first up, had forgotten to set her alarm clock, and was sleeping soundly when Mrs. Docker shook her into startled wakefulness.

They had none of them as yet heard of the second tragedy that had occurred during the night — this news was to reach them later — and during their hasty preparations for breakfast they discussed the death of the chauffeur. Mrs. Docker had a theory that it was a tramp, and refused to listen to Nellie's wild suggestions of secret societies, and gangs of criminals.

Anne, a pale ghost of her former self, took no part in this heated argument, but went about her work in silence, her lips compressed and her face totally devoid of all expression.

She was carrying a tray into the dining room when Eustace called her from the head of the stairs.

'Anne! I say, Anne!'

She gave such a start at the sound of his voice that she almost dropped her burden.

'Oh,' she said breathlessly. 'You — you startled me, sir.'

Eustace was full of apologies.

'I'm so sorry,' he said. 'Really I didn't mean to frighten you. But have you seen my bath salts?'

'Aren't they in the bathroom, sir?' she asked looking up at him.

He shook his head, and pulled his dressing gown closer round him.

'Only the lavender ones, and I couldn't possibly use those,' he replied plaintively. 'I'm in a *Quelque Fleurs* mood this morning.'

'They must be somewhere, sir,' said Anne, resting her tray on the hall table. 'I haven't moved them.'

'What is it you want?' asked the sharp metallic voice of Georgina.

She had come quietly up behind her

118

son, and he turned to her and explained.

'I can't find my bath salts anywhere,' he said. 'You know, the new ones I bought the other day.'

'I don't suppose you can,' she replied. 'I've got them, and I'm going to keep them.'

She pushed past him and began to descend the stairs.

'Oh, but Mater,' he protested, 'that's too bad of you. I hadn't even opened them.'

'Well, you won't get the chance, now,' she snapped. 'I've left you some carbolic soap in their place.'

He gave a little squeal of horror.

'Carbolic soap,' he repeated pathetically.

'Yes,' said his mother sharply. '*I* use it.'

'But *I* couldn't,' he answered. 'My skin's far too tender.'

'Rubbish!' she retorted.

'But, Mater — ' he began and she made a gesture of impatience.

'Don't argue!' she said. 'Go along and wash yourself!'

He opened his mouth to reply, thought

better of it, and shrugged his shoulders resignedly.

'All right,' he said turning away with a sigh, 'but you've absolutely spoilt my day!'

She made no reply, but crossing the hall entered the dining room, and going over to the fire warmed her hands.

'Good morning, Anne,' she said as the housemaid began to lay the table. 'Am I the first down?'

'No, ma'am,' answered Anne. 'Mr. Fordyce and Mr. Wainwright are outside somewhere talking to Inspector Jukes.'

'Good gracious!' exclaimed Georgina frowning. 'Is that man still here?'

Anne nodded.

'I think he came back early this morning, ma'am,' she said.

'Well I hope they won't be long,' remarked Georgina. 'I'm hungry.'

Anne raised her head, and looked at her in faint surprise.

'Hungry, ma'am?' she said.

Georgina screwed her monocle into her eye, and thrust her hands into the pockets of her tweed jacket.

'Isn't this a very good time to be hungry?' she asked.

'But after what — what happened last night — ' Anne stopped, leaving her sentence unfinished, and Georgina shrugged her shoulders.

'My good girl, you surely don't expect me to starve myself because of that?' she said harshly. 'Somebody dies every minute.'

'Ordinary death, ma'am, yes,' said Anne, in a low voice. 'But not — not murder.'

'All forms of death are unpleasant — ' began Georgina, and stopped as Peggy came in.

'Good morning, Georgina,' she said and nodded to Anne.

Her eyes were tired, and there were dark circles beneath them, which showed up with startling cleanness against the pallor of her face.

'Hello, Margaret,' greeted the elder woman. 'You're looking pretty rotten.'

'I've got rather a headache,' answered the girl listlessly.

'A cup of tea and a good breakfast will soon cure that,' said Georgina.

'I'd love the tea,' answered Peggy, 'but I

don't think I could manage to eat anything.'

She came over to the fireplace.

'Did you manage to get any sleep?'

'Of course I did,' said Georgina. 'I slept
like a top for nearly five hours.'

'I didn't,' said Peggy, looking at her in
wonder. 'You must have very strong nerves.'

'It's got nothing to do with nerves,
child,' replied Georgina. 'It's just a total
lack of imagination.'

'I was just dropping off once,' said
Peggy, 'when I heard somebody moving
about downstairs, and a muffled sound
like the closing of a door — '

'For Heaven's sake, don't let's get on
the subject of noises again, Margaret,'
said Georgina, irritably. 'I've had quite
enough of that last night.'

She looked across at Anne. 'How long
will breakfast be, Anne?'

'I'm just going to bring it now, ma'am,'
replied the housemaid, and as she was
leaving the room John and Wainwright
entered.

They looked surprised at seeing Peggy
and Georgina.

'I didn't expect there'd be anyone up yet,' said John, and Peggy noticed that he was looking worried and shaken.

'You two were up early,' remarked Georgina, 'and I hear you have already been communing with the law.'

Wainwright nodded.

'He's come back, then?' said Peggy.

'Yes, he's come back,' answered John, gravely. 'We had to send for him.'

He looked from one to the other and moistened his lips.

'You see there's been another murder.'

Peggy uttered a little exclamation of horror.

'Another — murder?' she repeated. 'Who — who was it?'

'Nobody we know,' put in Wainwright, quickly. 'A Scotland Yard man called Blackwood.'

'A detective?' breathed the girl, and he answered in the affirmative. 'But what was a detective doing here?' she went on. 'I suppose it — it did happen here?'

'Near the gate at the end of the drive,' answered Wainwright. 'We don't know what he was doing here. That's one of the mysteries that have to be solved.'

'And some people say living in the country is dull!' remarked Georgina.

At that moment Anne came in with the breakfast, and they were silent until she had gone. Only Wainwright and Georgina made a pretence of eating. John and Peggy contented themselves with a cup of tea and a small piece of dry toast.

'It doesn't seem real to me,' said the girl in a whisper as she sipped her tea gratefully. 'It's like a nightmare.'

'I'm afraid it's real enough,' answered John. 'Who would have thought that anything like this would have happened here.'

'What's the inspector doing?' enquired Georgina, her mouth full of egg and bacon.

'He's gone back to the station,' answered Wainwright, 'but I don't think we've got rid of him for long.'

'Was this man — this detective — killed in the same way as Gore?' asked Peggy.

John nodded.

'Yes,' he said. 'It's my belief there's a lunatic at large. That's the only thing I can think of to account for these killings.'

'What about the message and the noises in the night?' said Wainwright stretching out his hand for a piece of toast. 'Your lunatic idea doesn't account for them.'

John made a gesture of despair.

'I can't think of any reasonable explanation,' he said. 'Why should any sane person want to kill Gore, and if anybody did want to kill him, why should they have done it in the way they did?'

'What is Inspector Jukes' theory?' asked Peggy, and John screwed up his face in a grimace of disgust.

'I don't think he's got a theory,' he answered. 'The best thing that can happen is for them to call in Scotland Yard, and if the Chief Constable's got any sense, that's what he'll do.'

'I think you underrate Jukes' intelligence,' remarked Wainwright. 'I don't think he's nearly such a fool as he looks.'

'I should think it would be impossible,' grunted Georgina.

'Well, we haven't seen much proof of his intelligence up to now,' said John sarcastically. 'Perhaps that is a treat in store — '

He broke off and stood listening. The faint sound of a car engine reached their ears, growing louder as it came up the drive.

'Who the deuce can that be?' muttered John. 'It can't be Jukes. He hasn't had time to get to Tor Bridge and back.'

Peggy, who had gone over to the window, turned suddenly.

'It's Frank!' she cried, and ran out into the hall to meet the newcomer.

11

Simon Talbot

Frank Elford's arrival that morning had been purely accidental, and the result of a sudden caprice. At eleven o'clock on the preceding night, he had not had the faintest intention of going to Devonshire. It was not until he had left the offices of the *Morning Sun,* and was contemplating going home, that a sudden ridiculous desire to see Peggy again attacked him. He was used to acting on impulse, and an hour later he had got out his little car and started on the preliminary stage of his long journey.

He listened aghast at the news they had to tell him.

'Good Heavens, how dreadful!' he said. 'I knew Blackwood quite well.'

His first thought, after he had recovered from the momentary shock, was for his paper. A good reporter puts his paper before everything else, and Frank Elford was a very good reporter indeed, in spite of the occasional acrid comments, which a tired and irritable news editor fired at him. When he had expressed his sympathy with the household, he began to question John concerning what had actually happened, and in half an hour had succeeded in worming a sufficiently detailed story to phone through to the *Morning Sun*.

He came back from the telephone, his face wreathed in smiles.

'I'm 'covering' the crimes,' he said. 'Can you manage to put me up, or would you rather I went over to the hotel at Tor Bridge?'

Neither John nor Peggy would hear of his leaving.

'Only too glad to have you,' said John, and he meant it. 'Perhaps you'll be able to get to the bottom of this business. Until it's all finished and done with, life's going to be impossible.'

'You can bet I shall do my best,' said Frank. 'It's going to be a big story, and if I can get the 'why' and 'how' of it, it'll be a scoop for the *Sun*.'

He demanded to be shown the scene of the second murder, and John and Wainwright took him down to the place. The body had been removed, but the broken branches and stained leaves of the bushes were eloquent testimony to the tragedy that had occurred.

Frank asked innumerable questions and was particularly interested in the man who had been seen in the drive, and the noises in the night.

'I wonder if this business has got anything to do with your uncle?' he said suddenly as they were walking back to the house.

John pursed his lips thoughtfully.

'The idea hadn't occurred to me,' he replied, 'but I can't very well see how it could.'

'It's only a suggestion of mine,' said Frank, 'and I must admit that I've got no basis for making it. But it certainly seems to me as if this business was connected with the house, and since it's got nothing to do with you, it seems only logical to suppose that it's to do with the previous tenant.'

'It's fairly obvious,' put in Wainwright

quietly, 'that this masked man who has been lurking about the drive at night is after something inside the house. I think that accounts for his attempt to break in. If that's the case, it also explains the warning message which went astray.'

'How do you mean?' asked John.

'I mean,' answered Wainwright, 'that the burglary having failed, our friend, the man outside thought he would try and frighten you away. Once the house was unoccupied, he would be able to search for what he wants at his leisure.'

'But what does he want?' demanded John, and Wainwright shrugged his shoulders.

'Can't you suggest anything?' he asked. 'Did your uncle leave anything in the house of value?'

John shook his head.

'There are plenty of valuables,' he said, 'in the way of silver and whatnot, but nothing that I would consider worth taking all this trouble for.'

'No papers, or anything like that?' said Frank.

'No,' answered John. 'Homer, the solicitor, removed all my uncle's private papers when he came down immediately after his death.'

'Well, it's all very mysterious,' remarked the reporter. 'I'd like to have a chat to this fellow, Jukes. When's he coming back?'

'I'm expecting him at any time,' answered John.

They had reached the house by now, and Frank left them to talk to Peggy. He found the girl by herself in the drawing room, and she greeted him with a smile of pleasure.

'Well, have you seen all the exhibits?' she asked, and he nodded. 'It's dreadful isn't it, Frank?' she went on seriously. 'It was so pleasant and peaceful down here, and now everything seems to have been turned upside down.'

'It must be pretty rotten for you,' he admitted sympathetically.

'It's horrible,' she said with a shiver. 'I don't think I shall ever be able to feel really comfortable here again. Ever since last night I seem to have been living in an atmosphere of terror. I dread the thought of the night.'

'You mustn't get like that,' he said

practically. 'You must get a grip on your nerves. After all, you're in no danger.'

She swung round on him quickly.

'How can you be sure of that?' she said. 'How do you *know* that? There was danger for Gore, wasn't there? There was danger for the detective. Why shouldn't there be danger for all of us?'

He was silent, and she went on:

'It's the unknown that I'm afraid of. I don't mind anything that I can understand. It's the knowledge that somewhere near there is someone watching and waiting and planning. That's what terrifies me.' She stopped suddenly and abruptly and forced a smile. 'I'm talking an awful lot of nonsense, aren't I?' she said ruefully.

'I don't think you're talking nonsense at all,' he answered. 'I understand exactly how you feel.'

She went over to a box on the table, and helped herself to a cigarette.

'I envy Georgina,' she said. 'She's got nerves of steel.'

Frank took a lighter from his pocket, flicked it open, and held the flame to the end of her cigarette. 'Who is this fellow Wainwright?' he asked. 'What's he doing here?'

She blew a cloud of smoke from between her lips.

'Don't you remember Harry Wainwright?' she answered. 'He used to be at school with John.'

'I don't think I ever met him then,' he said shaking his head. 'But I've met him somewhere since, and I can't remember where. His face is terribly familiar.'

Before she could reply there came a sound of voices in the hall, and she looked towards the door.

'That's Inspector Jukes back again,' she said a little wearily.

'I want to see him,' said Frank. 'Do you mind if I go and have a chat to him?'

She shook her head, and he went out into the hall. Inspector Jukes was accompanied by a stout man of military appearance with a reddish face and grey moustache. They were both talking to John, and the inspector broke off in the middle of what he was saying and looked at Elford enquiringly as he came over to them. John introduced the reporter, and the expression on Jukes' face was anything but pleased. The red-faced man was Colonel Hodgkins, the Chief Constable for the county, and his greeting was more genial.

'This is an extraordinary business,' he said, in a slightly husky voice, though whether this was from the effect of a slight cold or the means by which he had acquired his florid complexion, Frank was unable to make up his mind. 'How did you get to hear of it so quickly?'

'I didn't know anything about it until I got here this morning.' replied Frank. 'But naturally I'm very interested. I shall be very glad if you can give me any inside information as to what the police are doing.'

'We've no information to give for publication at the moment,' grunted Jukes a little shortly. 'When we have I'll let you know.'

But Frank was too old a hand to be put off so easily.

'I naturally shouldn't publish anything without your permission,' he said, 'but at the same time I should like to keep in touch with your investigations. You see, apart from a professional interest in this affair, Blackwood was a friend of mine.'

The Chief Constable raised his rather bushy eyebrows.

'Oh, was he?' he replied. 'Have you any idea, then, why he was down here?'

Frank shook his head.

'No, I can't tell you that,' he said, 'but I've known him for some years. In fact I was with him on that case that got him his promotion. The robbery at Lowenstein and Marks. Do you remember it?'

'I believe I do remember something about it,' said Colonel Hodgkins, who obviously had not the faintest idea of what he was talking about, and abruptly changed the subject: 'That's what we're interested in at the moment. We've an idea that if we could find out why this man Blackwood was down here, it might give us a line to the other affair.'

'I should think they'd be able to tell you that at the Yard,' said Frank.

'I have already been in touch with them, sir,' put in Inspector Jukes, 'and apparently Detective-Inspector Blackwood came down yesterday to Princetown to interview the governor of the prison to get some information from a prisoner. The reason he was there can have nothing whatever to do with his death, or the murder of this man, Gore.'

'Still, it accounts for his presence in the neighbourhood,' said Frank.

The Chief Constable pursed his rather thick lips.

'It's a good step from Princetown to this house,' he remarked dubiously, 'and there seems no reason why he should have come all that way particularly so late at night.'

'Unless it was with the intention of coming here,' remarked the quiet voice of Harry Wainwright.

He had come softly out of the dining room and had heard Colonel Hodgkins' last remark.

'Why should he want to come here?' demanded John.

Wainwright shrugged his shoulders.

'I don't know,' he replied, 'unless it was in connection with the man in the drive.'

Inspector Jukes looked at him quickly.

'Are you suggesting, sir,' he said, 'that Blackwood knew about this man?'

'Yes,' answered Wainwright. 'It seems to me fairly plausible. He may have learned something about this fellow and been coming up to warn Mr. Fordyce, when he was killed.'

Jukes did not appear to attach much importance to this theory.

'It strikes me as being rather far fetched,' he remarked. 'It means that while Blackwood was down here on his own business he stumbled on the reason for this man hanging about the house, and it doesn't seem likely to me.'

'It's only a suggestion,' said Wainwright indifferently, 'and anyway you've got to account for Blackwood's presence here somehow. It's less likely that he would have been walking about in this vicinity in the rain for the sake of a constitutional.'

'The whole thing seems to me to boil down to this,' said Frank, 'the motive behind the killing of Gore. Once you've found that out, you'll probably find that everything else is clear.'

The Chief Constable nodded ponderously.

'I agree with you there,' he said, 'and I think Inspector Jukes is of that opinion too.'

He looked at the inspector for confirmation, and Jukes inclined his head.

'Yes, that's my opinion, sir,' he answered. 'And now if you don't mind I'd like to have a word with your kitchenmaid and be getting back. I've got a lot of work to do.'

John offered to ring for Nellie, but the inspector preferred to seek her out himself in the kitchen, and left them with this intention.

While he was gone they chatted to the Chief Constable. He was a bluff, hearty man, who obviously rather hated the business on which he was engaged, and was much more inclined to talk about the neighbourhood, and the people who lived there, than the sinister business which was the reason for his presence.

It was Frank who brought the conversation back to the matter in hand.

'Would you have any objection,' he said

suddenly, breaking into the Colonel's account of a dinner party he had been at on the previous night, 'to my dropping into the mortuary, and seeing the body of Gore?'

'Eh?' Colonel Hodgkins looked at him with surprised blue eyes. 'Not at all, my dear fellow. I'll arrange it with Jukes.'

He returned to his story, which was rather a dull one, and had just reached the uninteresting climax when the inspector returned.

The Chief Constable put forward Frank's request, and suggested that he should return with Jukes then. The inspector was not at all enthusiastic, but he agreed with as good a grace as possible.

The road to Tor Bridge ran straight across the open moor, before it turned off half a mile outside the small town.

Jukes drove in silence, and although Frank tried to make conversation for the first part of the journey, the other only answered in monosyllables, and he gave it up.

The mortuary at Tor Bridge was really a large shed adjacent to the tiny police station, and the inspector stopped the car outside this and getting out, fumbled in his pocket for a key. He found it, and unlocking the door, held it open for Frank to enter.

The interior of the building was dark and cold, what little light there was percolated through a dirty skylight in the roof, but this was sufficient to show the reporter the long trestle table with its sheeted burden.

Jukes closed the door, and pressing a switch flooded the place with the cold hard light of a naked electric bulb.

'Now, sir,' he said ungraciously, 'this is the dead man, Gore.'

In the more powerful light of the bulb, Frank saw that the trestle table contained two figures lying side by side covered by a single sheet, and as Jukes crossed over and pulled down the covering from the nearest of these, Frank followed him up, and stared down at the white set face, and staring, he suddenly held his breath, while a curious expression crept into his face.

'Is that Gore?' he asked in a low voice.

The inspector nodded.

'That's Gore,' he grunted. 'Have you seen all you want?'

He was pulling the sheet back, when Frank laid a detaining hand on his arm.

'You may have known him as Gore,' he said, 'but that's not his real name. His real name is Simon Talbot, and he's the man who was responsible for the robbery at Lowenstein and Marks five years ago!'

12

The Secret Drawer

John Fordyce stood by the library window, and gazed out at the fading day. His thoughts were very nearly as gloomy as the weather outside, for the morning, which had started so brightly had given place to grey rain clouds, and there was every prospect of the coming night being a wet one.

The vivid stain on the carpet was only faintly visible, for with the aid of soap and water, a protesting and shivering Nellie had managed to remove the worst of it. But its faint outline was still there, a tangible reminder, if he needed one, of the tragedy that had occurred on the previous night. He was feeling disconsolate and a little irritable. Frank Elford had not returned for luncheon, rather to his surprise, and immediately after the meal, Harry Wainwright had disappeared somewhere, so that John had been left to himself, for Georgina and Eustace had decided to go for a walk, and Peggy had gone up to her room to try and make up a little of the sleep she had lost.

He turned away presently from the unprepossessing prospect that the view from the window presented, and coming over to the fireplace poked the fire into a blaze, and dropped into an easy chair. Lighting a cigarette, he leaned back and allowed his thoughts to wander over the series of incidents, which had culminated in such a startling and unexpected denouement. What was at the bottom of these two crimes that had upset the smoothness of their lives and turned the house from a place of delight into a gloomy edifice of terror?

Who was this man who had suddenly made his appearance, and evinced such an interest in the house? Why had he tried to break in on that night when he had been surprised by Peggy, and, above all, why had he killed Gore and the Scotland Yard man? Try as he would, John could find no reasonable answer to these questions. It suddenly struck him that so far as the last was concerned, he was only acting on an assumption. There was no definite proof that the masked man had committed the murders. It was a reasonable assumption certainly, taking everything into consideration, but purely an assumption for all that. One thing, however, was definite. This man who lurked about in the drive was after something inside the house. Setting aside the remote possibility that he was just an ordinary burglar, that was the only explanation. But what could it be that he wanted so badly, and was there any connection between his attempt to break in, and the mysterious noises, which had been heard in the night? Was it possible that that attempt which had been frustrated by Peggy had not been the first, and that the others had been more success-ful? Was it this mysterious stranger, seeking for the thing he sought, that had been the cause of the tapping and the shuffling footsteps?

John flung his half-smoked cigarette into the fire, and unconsciously shook his head. If he had succeeded in getting into the house, there would surely have been some traces of this entry. Unless, and here a startling thought occurred to him, someone inside the house had been acting in collusion with him and let him in. He wondered if he had by accident hit upon something important. Was it possible that Gore had been the masked man's accomplice in this respect, and that his death had been the result of some quarrel between them? It was certainly a plausible theory, though it offered no suggestion as to what it was that the man was searching for. It could be nothing that either he or Peggy had brought to the house, he was sure of that. And therefore, it must be something that was already in the house when they arrived. But in this case, why couldn't the man who was after it, whatever it was, have taken advantage of the period when the place was uninhabited, when he could have searched to his heart's content without risk of being disturbed? This was rather a facer, and John spent a lot of time trying to find a solution, but without result, and eventually he went back to the subject of what it was the man was after.

Since it must have been in the house before he and Peggy had come to live there, it must be connected with his uncle. Now what could the old man have possessed that was worth all this trouble to try and obtain?

Mentally he went over a list of all the things he knew to be in the house, but there was not, so far as he could see, a single one that would warrant anybody talking a risk to get hold of it. Therefore the thing this man was after was something that he — John — did not know about.

Perhaps the old man had hidden something. Yet if he had, how had this unknown individual become aware of the fact? John suddenly remembered that there had been two old servants who had attended to his uncle's wants. Was it possible that these two could be mixed up in the business? If the old man had hidden anything in the home, they were the most likely to have known about it, but since his death they had completely disappeared, and John had no knowledge of their whereabouts. Probably Mr.

Homer, the solicitor, would know, and he determined to ask him at the first opportunity. What could it be, if anything, that the old man had hidden?

Obviously it must be something very valuable, but what? It might be money. According to Mr. Homer, Grant had been rather eccentric, and he had met his death suddenly, before he would have had time to have made any arrangements concerning any hidden hoard. He had had no time to even speak, the car which had killed him had killed him instantly. The more John thought of it, the more it seemed to him to be likely that the old man had concealed somewhere in the house a large sum of money, and that it was this that the man in the drive was after.

He rose to his feet, and began pacing up and down, his mind still working busily round this hypothesis. The grey light of the afternoon had faded rapidly to darkness — and he paused by the desk to switch on the shaded lamp. He felt pretty sure that he was on the right track, and experienced a little glow of self-complacency. He had, at least, a tangible suggestion to put up to Wainwright and Elford when they came back, and in this respect, his afternoon had not been wasted.

He went over the thing again carefully, clarifying his original theory, until he had got it cut and dried. There was no doubt that it was the most feasible explanation to account for the chain of events that had happened that had yet offered itself. There was only one stumbling block, and this he found impossible to overcome. Why hadn't the attempt been made to get this money, or whatever it was, while the house had been empty? There was one answer to this, but John thought it was rather a feeble one. And that was, that these people had not become aware of the existence of the thing they were after until he and Peggy had moved in.

He decided to suggest to the others that they should make a thorough search of the house to try and find this hidden fortune of old Grant's. He had definitely made up his mind that it was either money or something equally valuable that lay concealed within the walls of Raven

House. There was, he remembered, rolled up in a drawer of the desk, a plan of the building. He had found it when he had been arranging his own papers, and had pushed it to the back and left it there, Coming over to the desk, he sat down and pulled open the drawer.

The plan was still there, and spreading it out on the blotting pad, he studied it carefully. When he had seen it before, he had only given it the merest glance. At that time it hadn't particularly interested him. But now he went over every line of the drawing in the hope that it might afford some clue to a hiding-place.

But there was nothing extraordinary about it, and he soon came to the conclusion that it wasn't likely to afford any help at all. Now that he came to look at it more closely, he saw that it was not even a complete plan of the house. It only contained those additions that had been built on to the original building.

He rolled it up and put it back again where he had found it, and he was in the act of rising to his feet when a fresh thought struck him. The desk, unlike the rest of the furniture, was very modern. It was a huge roll top affair made of solid oak, quite an expensive piece of furniture And the thought that had suddenly occurred to John was that, perhaps here there might be something that he had previously overlooked. He had had a desk very similar to this in Canada, and he remembered that behind the long narrow drawers on each side under the nest of pigeon holes there had been a concealed drawer.

If such was the case with this desk, it might very easily contain the clue he was seeking. He pulled out the drawers on the left, and felt about in the cavity revealed gingerly. But the woodwork was quite smooth, his fingers touched no little knob as had been the case with his Canadian desk. He put the drawers back, and pulled out the companion ones on the right hand side, and he had scarcely put his hand into the place where they had been before he found what he had been searching for.

At one side flush with the wood, his fingers came in contact with cold metal.

He pressed, there was a faint click, and part of the back of the desk jumped forward on a spring.

With hands that trembled with excitement he lifted the false back out, and saw behind it a long narrow drawer. He pulled this open and discovered inside an envelope. It was heavily sealed but bore no address, and breaking the seal, he ripped it open. It contained a single sheet of paper, covered in his uncle's neat careful writing. John read it, and as he read, his eyes opened wide with astonishment, for here was something that was totally unexpected, and made the mystery of Raven House even deeper still!

13

The Will

Inspector Jukes' small eyes widened, and he looked at Elford with an expression of astonishment.

'This is a very serious statement, sir, that you've made,' he said gravely. 'Are you sure you haven't made a mistake?'

The reporter shook his head emphatically.

'No, I've made no mistake, Inspector,' he declared. 'This man here is Simon Talbot. I'll show you why I'm so sure.' He leaned forward and pointed to a small, curiously shaped scar on the under part of the dead man's chin. 'I should have recognised him without this,' he went on, 'but this clinches the matter.'

Jukes rubbed his chin thoughtfully.

'Well, if you're sure, sir, that's all there is to it,' he said. 'I must admit that this identification is going to be of consider-able help. Perhaps you can give me some more information. About this robbery, for instance.'

'I can,' said Frank, 'and I will. But this is not a very comfortable place to talk in, can't we go somewhere else?'

'We'll go into my office at the station, sir,' answered the inspector.

He replaced the sheet over the waxen face of the dead man, and crossing over to the door, waited until Frank had passed out of the building, and then closed it and locked it behind him. They walked up the steps of the little police station, and entered the charge room. The desk sergeant looked up as they came in.

'Anything for me, Wilson?' asked Jukes.

The man shook his head.

'No, sir, nothing,' he replied.

'I don't want to be disturbed for the next hour,' said the inspector, and crossing the big bare room, opened a door in one corner.

'Come in, sir,' he said and ushered Frank into a small plainly-furnished office.

He pulled forward a chair for the reporter, and took his own place behind a shabby flat-topped desk.

'Now, sir,' he said, pulling a notebook towards him, and picking up a pencil. 'I'd like you to tell me all you know about this man Talbot.'

Frank considered a little while before he replied.

'I can only give you second-hand information,' he said at last. 'What I know about Simon Talbot I learned from Blackwood, whom I think I told you was a friend of mine. Talbot is, or rather was, a very well-known jewel thief; his speciality was diamonds, and because of this he was nicknamed 'Shiner' Talbot. His last big job was the robbery at Lowenstein and Marks, the jewellers, of Bond Street. But this time it wasn't diamonds he got away with, but emeralds. There was an Indian Rajah over in England on a visit, who wanted to take back an emerald necklace. He wanted it to be the most perfect one of its kind, and he commissioned old Marks to find the stones. To cut a long story short, Marks succeeded in getting together a collection of some of the finest emeralds in the world. An appointment was made with the Rajah to come and inspect the stones, but on the night before, Lowenstein and Marks' premises were broken into, the lock of the safe burnt out and the emeralds pinched. Blackwood, who was put on the case, told me that directly he saw that safe he knew that it was Shiner Talbot's work as surely as if he had signed his name. It was three weeks, however, before they got him, and even then there was no sign of the stones. He was questioned repeatedly both before and at his trial, but he steadfastly refused to say what had happened to them. The police tried all the known 'fences', but there was no trace of them, and they've never been found to this day ... As you know, an enquiry is never dropped at Scotland Yard, and Blackwood was always hoping that he would be able to discover the whereabouts of the stolen jewels. Talbot got five years — it wasn't his first sentence — he'd been convicted twice before. That's about all I can tell you, Inspector.'

Jukes frowned down at his notes.

'Well, it throws a different complexion on the matter,' he grunted. 'I wonder why this man, Talbot, took a position with Mr. Fordyce as chauffeur.'

'I'm afraid I can't tell you that,' answered Frank. 'But I should imagine that his death had something to do with these missing emeralds.'

The inspector took a packet of cheap cigarettes from his pocket, put one between his lips and lit it. Blowing out the smoke he leaned back in his chair and stared at the ceiling.

'Five years, eh,' he muttered thoughtfully. 'He couldn't have been out so very long, even if he earned his full remission for good conduct. H'm, well I'm very much obliged to you, Mr. — '

'Elford,' said Frank.

'Elford,' repeated the inspector, 'and I'll follow this information up. I suppose there's nothing else you can tell me?'

'No, I don't think so,' replied the reporter. 'If you do get hold of anything, you might let me know.'

Jukes nodded slowly.

'I will,' he said, and Frank rose to his feet.

'Can I publish this information?' he

asked, 'that Gore was really Shiner Talbot?'

The inspector considered this request for some time.

'I don't see that it can do any harm,' he remarked at length. 'I shall get on to the Yard to see what further information they can give me about the man.'

Frank left him to attend to his business, for he had plenty of his own to look after, and his first move on leaving the police station at Tor Bridge was to hire a car from the one garage the little town boasted, and drive over to Princetown.

He had some difficulty in getting an interview with the governor of the prison, but he succeeded eventually, and an hour's conversation with that surprised man put him in possession of several facts that he needed.

From the prison he drove to the post office, and put through a call to the *Morning Sun* offices, after which he went to an hotel and had something to eat. For the remainder of the afternoon he was busily occupied at Tor Bridge, and it was dark by the time he got back to Raven House.

As Anne let him in, Peggy was coming down the stairs. She stopped as she saw him.

'Hello, Frank,' she said. 'where have you been?'

'Very busy,' he answered briefly, coming to the foot of the staircase and looking up at her. 'You look very nice.'

She glanced down at herself and smoothed her dress.

'This is rather an adorable frock, isn't it?' she answered.

'I wasn't referring to the frock,' he retorted. 'You'd look just as nice without it.'

'Don't be vulgar,' she said severely.

'I'm not,' he protested. 'You know perfectly well what I mean.'

She came a few steps farther down.

'Tell me what you've been doing all day,' she asked.

'I've been collecting information for my paper,' he answered; and then suddenly, 'Peggy, do you know why I came down here?'

She knew perfectly well, but her expression of surprise was very convincing.

'No, why?' she asked innocently.

'Because I wanted to see you,' he answered.

She raised her eyebrows.

'I see,' she replied. 'That's why you spent practically the whole day somewhere else?'

He made a gesture of impatience.

'You know it isn't,' he said. 'But I never expected to land in the middle of a murder mystery. After all, I'm a reporter, and I must consider my paper.'

She looked at him quizzically.

'Have you finished considering it, now then?' she asked.

'Yes, for the time being,' he answered. 'And now I want to talk to you.'

She made him a little mock curtsey.

'Well, here I am,' she said coolly. 'what have you got to say to me?'

She intended to descend the rest of the stairs with quiet dignity, but unfortunately for this intention she caught the heel of one of her shoes at the first step and slithered down the rest into Elford's arms. He held her for a moment, and then suddenly bending forward kissed her full on the lips.

159

'That's what I've got to say to you!' he said a little breathlessly.

'Frank!' she gasped and struggled to free herself, but he held her more closely and kissed her again recklessly.

'You darling!' he said, 'When we're married — '

She pushed him away, her face a little flushed, and patted her disordered hair.

'You're rather rushing things, aren't you?' she demanded. 'You haven't even asked me yet.'

He grinned.

'I thought I'd made it fairly obvious,' he retorted.

'It's rather like being proposed to in shorthand,' she answered.

'Well, of course,' he began, 'if you prefer — '

Leaving the sentence unfinished, he took a step towards her, but she backed away.

'Just because a girl allows you to kiss her,' she said demurely, 'you mustn't take it for granted that she's ready to rush into matrimony.'

'I always understood that it was a

necessary preliminary,' he retorted.

She shook her head primly.

'Not always,' she answered. 'If a girl married every man who kissed her, she'd have to spend the rest of her life in the Divorce Courts!'

He was not quite sure if she was serious or not, and looked a little disconcerted.

'I'm sorry if I jumped to conclusions,' he said rather stiffly.

'Of course,' said Peggy quickly, her eyes twinkling, 'there are some girls who wouldn't let a man kiss them unless — unless — '

'Unless what?' demanded Elford.

She came over to him, and without looking at him began to play with the lapel of his coat.

'I think for a reporter,' she said softly, 'you're rather dense . . . '

Georgina came out of the drawing room a minute later, and they hurriedly broke apart.

'Hello!' she said staring at them through her monocle. 'What are you two doing?'

'Frank has been talking about his

paper,' answered Peggy, and the elder woman's lips curled.

'I'd no idea,' she remarked acidly, 'that he had any connection with the *Matrimonial Post*!'

'What do you mean?' asked Peggy.

Georgina shrugged her shoulders.

'I don't know why you should pretend to be surprised,' she said. 'I suppose I ought to offer my congratulations.'

Elford looked at her in astonishment.

'How do you — ' he began.

'How do I know?' she interrupted quickly. 'My dear man, when a girl transfers half her complexion to the lapel of a man's coat, it's absurd to expect one to believe that they have been discussing the weather.'

'Damn!' exclaimed Frank looking down, and then: 'I beg your pardon. I never noticed that.'

'You're lucky, Margaret,' said Georgina. 'That's a sure sign he's inexperienced.'

Before the girl could reply, the library door opened, and John appeared on the threshold. He was carrying a paper in his hand, and he looked excited. Catching sight of Frank, he called to him.

'I say, Elford!' he said, 'I've made a discovery.'

The reporter went over to him quickly. 'What is it?' he asked.

Fordyce explained.

'When I opened the secret drawer,' he concluded, 'I found this inside in an envelope.'

He handed Frank the sheet of paper he had been holding in his hand, and as the reporter read the first words, his lips pursed into a silent whistle.

'What is it?' asked Peggy interestedly at his elbow.

'It's a will,' answered Frank, and read slowly from the document:

'This is the last will and testament of me, William Grant, of Raven House, in the county of Devon, made this day of September in the year of Our Lord one thousand, nine hundred and thirty-two. I give and bequeath unto my nephew, John Fordyce, at present abroad, or if he should die before the occurrence of my death, unto his sister Margaret, the whole of my estate both real and personal, with the exception of Raven House and all therein contained. This, I give and bequeath unto Simon Talbot, now serving a term of imprisonment for robbery at His Majesty's convict prison at Princetown, and I wish to draw his special attention to the books contained on the top shelf of the right hand bookcase in my library. I hereby revoke all other wills and codicils made by me at any time heretofore.

(Signed) WILLIAM GRANT.
(Witnessed) MARTHA DRAGE.
THOMAS BATES.'

'That's a very interesting document, John,' said Wainwright's voice, as Elford finished reading. 'Most interesting!'

They looked round a little startled, and saw that he had come halfway down the stairs, and was leaning against the banisters.

'Hello, Harry,' said John. 'I'd no idea you were there.'

'I didn't want to interrupt,' replied Wainwright coming down the remainder of the flight and joining them.

'Well, what do you make of this, eh?' said John; he indicated the paper in Elford's hand. 'It seems to make the whole business more mysterious than ever.'

'I think it rather clears things up,' said Frank. 'This reference to Simon Talbot is a queer coincidence.'

He told them what he had discovered at Tor Bridge earlier in the day, and John was staggered.

'Good God!' he exclaimed. 'So that's who Gore was?'

'And you were never intended to have this house, John,' put in Wainwright. 'Your uncle made that will so that there should be no doubt about its passing into the possession of this man, Talbot, at his death.'

'But why did he want Talbot to have it?' asked Peggy, frowning.

'I don't think that's very difficult to guess,' answered Wainwright. 'Remember how the will reads: 'This house and all it contains',' He paused and repeated the last words slowly, looking from one to the other meaningfully.

'By Jove!' said Elford. 'You mean that — '

'I mean,' interrupted Wainwright, 'that Talbot took the position of chauffeur because there was something in the house he wanted. Something that only he and Grant knew was here.'

Peggy caught her breath.

'The emeralds!' she breathed softly, and Wainwright nodded.

14

The Books

They stood there outside the half open door of the library and stared at each other. It was John who at length broke the silence.

'Supposing it's true,' he said thoughtfully, 'and that Talbot was after these emeralds. How did they get here?'

'It seems pretty obvious,' answered Wainwright, 'that they were brought here by your uncle.'

John frowned.

'That's nonsense!' he said impatiently. 'My uncle could have had no connection with the robbery.'

'No,' agreed Wainwright. 'But he may have had a very close connection with Simon Talbot.'

'Why?' demanded John. 'What should he have in common with a jewel thief?'

'I don't know,' said Wainwright shrugging his shoulders. 'But he obviously knew him intimately, the will proves that.'

'The whole thing's inexplicable,' declared John with a gesture of despair, 'and I don't profess to understand it. I'd worked out a theory this afternoon that there was something hidden in the house, but I'd come to the conclusion that it was money. Of course, I knew nothing about the emeralds then.'

'We're not definitely certain that it's the emeralds now,' remarked Elford. 'It's only a supposition.'

'It's a supposition on a very solid basis,' said Wainwright. 'I'm pretty certain that those emeralds are somewhere in the house, and that Talbot was here to get them.'

'Then why didn't he?' demanded Georgina. 'He was here long enough, he had plenty of time.'

'He would have got them, if he'd known where they were,' answered Wainwright. 'But he didn't. He knew nothing of the existence of this will. No doubt, Grant drew this up with the intention of giving it into the care of his lawyers, and was prevented by his sudden and unexpected death. But I think we can be pretty sure that

Talbot was searching for the jewels; the tapping in the night and the shuffling footsteps were probably the noise he made during his search.'

'It all sounds very clever,' said Georgina, sceptically, 'but after all, it's only guesswork.'

'Supposing it's all true, and the emeralds are hidden in the house,' said Peggy, 'who is the masked man who is always lurking about in Beech Drive?'

It was Wainwright who answered her, and his face was very grave.

'He is the Great Unknown,' he said. 'The equation X. We can't give him a name, but he is certainly the man who killed Talbot, and also killed Blackwood.'

'But why?' demanded Elford in a puzzled tone. 'That's the biggest mystery, unless he's also after the emeralds.'

'I think it's more than likely that he is,' answered Wainwright, 'although I've no idea why he should have killed Talbot and Blackwood.'

Frank rubbed his chin. 'Well, we've got a little farther, anyway,' he said. 'That reference in the will to the books, I should think, must mean the place where the emeralds are hidden.'

'I wonder if it's as easy as that,' muttered Wainwright, thoughtfully. 'May I look at that document a minute?'

Frank, who was still holding the will, passed it over to him, and Wainwright scanned it swiftly.

'I wish to draw his special attention to the books on the top shelf of the right hand bookcase in my library,' he read aloud, and looked up, his eyes moving from one to the other. 'Suppose we have a look at that shelf, eh? Curiosity was always a weakness of mine.'

They went into the library, which was lighted dimly by the desk lamp. John, however, pressed the switch by the door, and the big room became brilliantly illuminated from the centre pendant.

The bookcases occupied the two recesses each side of the fireplace, and going over to the right hand one, they looked up at the shelf mentioned in the will. The bookcases were massive affairs, with leaded panes arranged in such a manner that each shelf could be separately locked. There was nothing very special about the particular shelf they were looking at to mark it out from any of the others. Dimly behind the glass covering they could see a row of books, which were apparently novels. Frank Elford dragged over a small occasional table, and being the least heavy of the party — with the exception of Peggy — mounted it gingerly and examined the shelf at closer quarters,

'It's locked,' he reported.

John took a bunch of keys from his pocket, selected one, and handed them up to Elford.

'That key opens all the cases,' he said, as Frank reached down and took the bunch.

The reporter tried it in the lock, but it refused to turn.

'It doesn't fit this one,' he said. 'It should be a much smaller key.'

John frowned.

'That's the only key I've ever had for the book shelves,' he replied. 'Try the others.'

Frank tried them each in turn but none of them fitted that particular lock.

'The only thing to do, is to force it open,' said Wainwright. 'Have you got a screwdriver handy, John?'

Fordyce nodded, and turned away, presently returning with a small case opener.

'I think this'll be better than a screwdriver,' he said, and Frank took it from his hand.

He had some little difficulty in forcing the lock, but eventually he succeeded, and lifted up the glass panel. It had stays at the side, which kept it raised, and he was about to pull out the books haphazardly when Wainwright uttered a warning.

'I should be careful, now, if I were you,' he said. 'Take out each book one at a time, and put it back exactly in the same place. We don't know what this reference to the books means, yet.'

Frank nodded and began methodically to remove the volumes one at a time. The first one was *Going Somewhere*, by Max Ewing. He looked inside, shook it, and handed it down to Wainwright for further examination while he carefully felt about in the place where it had been, but neither he nor Wainwright could find anything. The book was a very ordinary one, none of the pages were marked and there was nothing in the binding. Wainwright handed the book back, and Elford replaced it, pulling out number two. This was *The Rasp*, by Philip Macdonald, and again they found nothing behind it or in the book itself; which elucidated the cryptic message in the will. In this manner they went through the entire shelf, and when they had finished and all the books had been put back in their original order, they had to admit that they were no wiser than when they bad started.

'There's nothing here at all,' grunted Frank. 'If there ever was anything, Talbot must have found it in his search and taken it away.'

Wainwright shook his head in disagreement.

'He didn't do that,' he declared. 'If he'd found what he was looking for, he wouldn't have stopped here. No, there's something about those books that we haven't discovered yet. Some hidden message.'

His brows contracted with the concentration of his thoughts, and he frowned up at the bookshelf, as though he would compel it to give up its secret by sheer will power.

They were all so occupied trying to think out a solution to the problem which the dead William Grant had propounded, that they failed to notice the crouching figure that had slid into view outside the library window, and was standing almost invisible in the darkness, the eyes through the slits in the mask which concealed its face, watching intently their every movement.

Suddenly Wainwright uttered an exclamation, and the crouching shape of the man outside moved away into the shadows beyond the light from the window.

'Listen, I've got an idea! Give me a sheet of paper, John.'

John Fordyce went over to the desk, and came back with a writing pad. Wainwright took it and drew from his pocket a fountain pen.

'Now, Elford,' he said, 'read me out the titles of those books in the order in which they appear on the shelf.'

Frank did so, and Wainwright jotted them down. The list when he had finished it ran as follows:

Title	Author
Going Somewhere	MAX EWING
The Rasp	PHILIP MACDONALD
Susan Plays a Lone Hand	MONICA EWER
Gold Rim	IRENE RATHBONE
The Fourth Dagger	LUKE ALLAN
Infallible Witness	PETER LUCK
Wu Fang	ROLAND DANIEL
Pay Dirt	CHARLES F. SNOW
Before the Fact	FRANCIS ILES
Belle-Mere	KATHLEEN NORRIS
The Calendar	EDGAR WALLACE
Contango	JAMES HILTON
Malice Aforethought	FRANCIS ILES
A Final Chance	PAUL TRENT
Love Girl	MAY EDGINTON
Dead Man's Rock	'Q,'
The Snake Pit	SIGRID UNDSET
Liquid Shadows	G. U. ELLIS
Pattern of a Star	CONSTANCE M. EVANS
Public Faces	HAROLD NICOLSON

'Is that the lot?' asked Wainwright.

'That's the lot,' said Frank, cheerfully. 'What now?'

'Wait a minute,' said Harry, and pen in hand he stared down at the list he had just made. At the expiration of five minutes he looked up.

'I think I've got it,' he said quietly, and there was a gleam of triumph in his eyes.

'What is it?' asked John, and Wainwright ran his pen swiftly through certain words on the list before him.

They clustered round him, and Frank in his eagerness, almost fell off the table on which he had been standing. The list as amended by Wainwright now ran:

Ewing
Macdonald
Ewer
Rathbone
Allan
Luck
Daniel
Snow
Iles
Norris

Wallace
Hilton
Iles
Trent
Edginton
'Q'
Undset
Ellis
Evans
Nicolson

'There you are,' said Wainwright. 'There's your message as plain as a pikestaff.'

John stared at it, and shook his head.

'I can't see any message,' he grunted. 'All you've done is to cross out the title of the book and the Christian name of the author.'

'I know I have,' retorted Wainwright, 'they aren't necessary. It's the author's surname we want, or rather the initial letter of it. Look!' he scribbled on the paper in front of him:

'E-M-E-R-A-L-D-S-I-N-W-H-I-T-E-Q-U-E-E-N.'

'There's your message. 'Emeralds in White Queen'.'

15

The White Queen

'By Jove!' exclaimed Frank Elford. 'That's a clever idea. How did you spot it?'

'More by luck than anything else,' answered Wainwright candidly. 'I was wondering if there might not be some sort of message hidden in the titles of the books, and quite accidentally while I was looking for something of the sort, saw that the initial letters of the authors' surnames reading from top to bottom made a sensible message.'

'But what does 'White Queen' mean?' asked Peggy, wrinkling her brows.

Wainwright shook his head.

'I don't know, I haven't got that yet,' he replied. 'Perhaps it refers to the title of another book.'

'I should think it's more likely to refer to a chess piece,' remarked Georgina, and John uttered an exclamation.

'I believe you're right,' he said excitedly. 'There's a set of chess men in the drawing room. Rather a beautiful set, I remember looking at them when we first moved in.'

'That's probably what Grant was referring to,' said Wainwright. 'Let's go and see.'

Followed by the others he hurried out of the library, and the crouching figure of the man outside the window, who had been intently watching their every movement, and striving vainly to hear what was being said, saw them go.

Beneath the silken covering that concealed his face, his lips set in a hard thin line. It was vital that he should know what had taken place in that room. He had not been able to catch even a stray word, for although he had strained his ears, nothing had reached him except a vague murmur of voices. From their actions he had guessed that they had made some kind of discovery, and he was pretty certain that it was connected with the emeralds. But in some way he must find out exactly what it was. His brows drew together in a frown as he cautiously peered into the now empty room. In the hurry of their departure they had left the door wide open, and he was able to see them cross the hall and enter the drawing room. Why had they gone there, he wondered. It was necessary that he should find out, and making up his mind, he hurried round the house until he came to the drawing room window on the opposite side.

The curtains here had been drawn, but they did not quite meet, and through the chink that remained he was able to get a fairly good view of the room. He saw John Fordyce go over to a table by the fireplace, lift up a large oak box, and carry it back to a larger table in the centre of the room.

The others crowded round him as he opened the box, and the watching man's breath quickened as he saw him begin to lift out a set of large beautifully carved chessmen. In a flash he understood what was happening, and began to think rapidly. He had very little time to lose, whatever he did, must be done quickly, all that he had waited and planned for might be put beyond his reach for ever, unless he acted now.

He came to a decision, and hurried back again to the library window. With hands that were shaking a little with the excitement he was feeling, he took from a pocket beneath his long coat a clasp knife, and opening it, inserted the long thin blade between the window frames near the hasp. Working quickly but carefully, he forced up the blade until he had succeeded in raising the catch. If the window had been bolted he would have had all his trouble for nothing, but it wasn't.

A little sigh of thankfulness escaped him as it opened under the pressure of his hand.

His forehead was damp with perspiration, and the blood in his veins was racing, as he cautiously stepped across the threshold and closed the window behind him. For a moment he stood listening, his eyes fixed on the oblong of the open door, through which he could see the hall, and the partly open door of the drawing room. He was taking a big risk, for if anybody should happen to come out into the hall they could not fail to see him.

But except for the almost inaudible mutter of voices that came from the drawing room there was no sound. With every sense alert he moved forward, creeping towards the door, step by step, pausing at every third pace to listen.

His right hand, thrust into the pocket of his overcoat, closed round the cold, hard butt of an automatic pistol, and the feel of it gave him confidence. If by any chance he should be surprised, he would have not the slightest compunction in using the weapon. Capture meant death on the gallows, and he had no intention of standing on the trap and toeing the chalk mark in the grey light of an early morning. He reached the hall without discovery, and after a quick glance left and right moved over to the drawing room.

Bending forward, he listened, and what he heard brought a cold glitter to his eyes. Swiftly he straightened up, and looking quietly about him began to move rapidly and noiselessly towards the shadows at the side of the staircase. Here he stopped and looked up at the wall. He found what he had hoped and expected to find, and with great care he pulled forward a chair and mounted it . . .

John Fordyce bent over the oak box that stood on the centre table in the drawing room, and carefully lifted out its contents. They were a set of very large chessmen, and from the carving, appeared to be of Chinese workmanship. They were obviously antiques, and would have fetched a considerable sum at any auction room. The White Queen, which was almost the last piece he brought to light, stood nearly eight inches high, a regal figure complete with crown and flowing robes. The workmanship was exquisite. Every little detail had been beautifully wrought by the hand of the carver.

John held the piece to his ear, and shook it gently. There was no sound from within, but when he balanced it in his hand and compared it with the weight of the Red Queen, there was a marked difference. It was definitely heavier.

He examined it carefully while the

others crowded round, their faces tense with suppressed excitement, but so far as he could see, there was no join anywhere in the figure, and no means by which anything could have been introduced into the interior. He said as much to Wainwright, and Harry reached over and took the figure from his hand.

'There must be some means of opening it,' he said. 'That is if we've read this message correctly, and I don't think there can be much doubt of that.'

He tried twisting the head this way and that, but nothing happened. It had, apparently, been carved from a solid block of ivory, which was yellow with age, and although he tapped it, and tried every means of discovering its secret, he had to admit at last, that it was beyond him.

'Let me look,' said Elford, holding out his hand.

Wainwright gave him the figure, and the reporter turned it this way and that in an endeavour to discover the means by which it opened.

'There must be something in it,' said John, 'otherwise it wouldn't be heavier than the other queen.'

'I think the only way you'll find out for certain,' said Elford, 'is to break it.' And Peggy made a little moue of protest.

'It's such a lovely thing, it would be a pity to do that,' she said.

'I'm afraid we shall have to if we can't find any other way,' grunted John. We must — '

'Just a minute,' interrupted Grant, 'has anyone got a pin?'

Peggy supplied him with a small brooch, and with the gold pin of this he gently probed an almost invisible hole at the apex of the crown. Without warning the bottom of the figure fell out, and dropped with a clatter on to the table.

'That's got it!' cried Elford excitedly, and turning the carving upside down, he pulled from the hollow interior a wad of cotton wool.

As he did so the light above was reflected in flashing green points of fire from the cavity revealed. He cupped his hand, and as he shook the figure of the White Queen gently over it, a stream of blazing green trickled out into his palm, and Peggy gave a little cry of delight.

'Oh, aren't they lovely!' she breathed.

They were lovely, thirty picked emeralds ranging in size from a hazel nut to a pea. They sparkled and flashed in the light like liquid green fire.

'Well there's no doubt now,' said Wainwright, 'what it was that Talbot was looking for. At a rough guess I should think those must be worth something like £200,000.'

'Quite that,' grunted Georgina, and her hard, metallic voice was not quite as steady as usual. 'I know something about emeralds, and they're the finest I've ever seen.'

Frank Elford poured them carefully out of his hand on to the table.

'Eventually,' he said, 'they'll have to go back to Lowenstein and Marks, but in the meantime what are we going to do with them?'

'I think,' suggested Wainwright, 'that for the moment we'd better put them back in the White Queen. Tomorrow we can — '

So far he got, when every light in the room went out!

16

The Man in the Dark

Peggy screamed as the room became plunged in darkness, and John uttered a startled exclamation.

'What's gone wrong with the lights?' he muttered angrily. 'They must have gone out all over the house, because the light in the hall's gone out too.'

He took one step towards the door, and then out of the darkness came a spear of light.

'Don't move, any of you!' said a high-pitched squeaky voice. 'You can't see the pistol in my hand, but you can take my word it's there!'

Frank Elford heard Wainwright draw in his breath sharply. The light that held them in its ray came from an electric torch, and it dazzled their eyes so that they could see nothing that was behind it.

'What's all this tomfoolery — ?' began

John irritably, but the voice of the unknown interrupted him.

'There's no tomfoolery,' it said, and the tone was menacing, 'as you'll find out if you don't do as you're told. You've got something there that I want. Give them to me!'

'Who are you?' snapped John.

'Never mind who I am,' retorted the voice coolly, 'it's what I want you've got to attend to, and I want those emeralds.'

'Don't be a fool!' broke in Wainwright sharply. 'You dare not shoot. It would — '

'Unless you hand over those stones,' went on the voice behind the torch relentlessly, 'I shall fire at the girl, and I warn you I shall shoot to kill!'

Frank Elford felt himself go suddenly cold, and the perspiration broke out on his forehead.

'For God's sake, let him have them, Wainwright!' he muttered huskily.

'He's only bluffing,' said Wainwright. 'I tell you he dare not — '

'I shouldn't advise you to put it to the test,' said the voice harshly. 'I'll give you while I count three to get away from that table. If you haven't moved by then, I shall shoot the girl.'

'But — ' said John.

'You heard what I said,' interrupted the voice, and began counting. 'One-two — '

'He means it,' muttered Elford. 'It's madness to risk it!'

'Three!' said the voice of the unknown, and Wainwright called out quickly:

'All right! We'll give in!'

They backed away from the table out of the circle of light, and as they moved the man in the dark advanced. The light he carried was focused on the table, and now in its reflected light they could dimly see the figure that held the torch.

'Where are the stones?' he asked sharply, as he drew near the table.

'In the White Queen,' answered Wainwright, and the man laid the torch down on the table, and picked up the ivory figure in his gloved hand.

'Keep back over there,' he warned, and slipping the figure of the White Queen into his pocket picked up the torch again. 'I'm still covering the girl.'

He began to back slowly towards the

door, keeping the ray from his lamp playing on the others. When he reached the threshold he administered his final warning,

'If you're wise, you won't attempt to follow me. Remember what happened to Talbot and Blackwood!'

As he uttered the last word, the light of the torch went out, and a moment afterwards they heard the door pull shut.

'See if you can put the lights on again,' whispered Wainwright, urgently in the darkness.

John felt his way over to the switch.

'The switch is on,' he said. 'He must have pulled a fuse out.'

'Try the standard lamp, Frank,' said Peggy shakily. 'It's a separate connection.'

He went over to the big floor lamp in the corner, and twisted the switch. Immediately the darkness was dispersed with a soft glow of light.

'That's better,' said Wainwright. 'I never expected he'd take such a risk.'

'Who was it?' asked Peggy, her face white.

'Our friend; the man outside,' answered

Wainwright. 'Pleasant gentleman, isn't he?'

He broke off as there came from outside the sound of a hoarse cry of fear and pain.

'My God!' muttered Elford. 'What was that?'

He made a move towards the hall, but Peggy caught him by the arm, and it was Wainwright who was the first to reach the front door. As he raised his hand to the latch, somebody began pounding agitatedly on the knocker.

'Hello, there!' cried a voice hoarse with fear. 'Mr. Fordyce! Let me in!'

'Good Heavens it's Jukes!' exclaimed Wainwright and jerked open the door.

The inspector reeled into the dimly lit hall, for the only light came from the open door of the drawing room, and leant against the wall panting heavily.

'What's the matter?' asked Wainwright, for Jukes was hatless and his face was streaked with mud.

'I've been attacked,' jerked the inspector breathlessly. 'I was coming up the drive when somebody ran into me. I tried to stop him but he struck at me savagely with a knife. Look here!'

He held out a shaking hand, and Wainwright saw that the blood was pouring from a nasty cut in the wrist.

'You'd better have that seen to at once,' he said, and taking Jukes by the arm led him into the drawing room.

The inspector collapsed into a chair. His experience had obviously shaken him up, for his usual ponderous dignity had completely gone. John got some water and with the aid of a clean handkerchief Wainwright bathed the man's wound and roughly bound it up.

'Thank you, sir,' said Jukes gratefully, when this had been done. 'It was the masked man who did it. I only saw him for a second. But I recognised him from your description, sir.' He looked at John. 'Has anything been happening here?'

'Quite a lot,' said Wainwright grimly. 'We've had a most entertaining evening!'

Briefly he related to the wondering Jukes the finding of the will, their discovery of the emeralds in the White Queen, and the holdup by the unknown.

The inspector listened, his expression testifying to his amazement.

'Good God, sir!' he exclaimed when Wainwright had finished. 'This fellow doesn't suffer from lack of nerve! How did he get in?'

Wainwright shook his head.

'I don't know yet,' he said. 'We haven't had time to look.'

'It may be that somebody in the house let him in,' said Jukes, and before they could ask him the reason for his remark he rose to his feet. 'Before we go any further, I'll have a look round,' he said.

There was no need to look very far, for as he reached the hall accompanied by John and Wainwright, a cold draught of air coming from the open door of the library attracted their attention, and entering the dark room they discovered that the french window was half open.

'I wonder how he managed the light trick?' muttered Jukes. 'We can't do very much in the dark.'

'I think he must have pulled a fuse out,' said Wainwright. 'We can easily see.' He turned to John. 'Where's the fuse box for this floor?' he asked.

Fordyce explained, and leaving him with Jukes in the library, Wainwright went out into the hall. He found the fuse box and the chair that stood under it, and after a few moments search discovered the fuse itself lying on the floor. He picked it up and mounting the chair replaced it. The light sprang on as he did so, and when he got back to the library he found the inspector examining the catch of the window.

'This is how he got in,' he grunted, looking round. 'Forced up the catch with a knife or something similar. You can see the scratches plainly.' He straightened up and scratched his chin. 'Pity he got away with those emeralds,' he said.

'It would be a pity if he had,' answered Wainwright quietly, and Jukes looked at him sharply.

'What do you mean, if he had, sir?' he said. 'I thought you told me — '

'I told you he got away with the White Queen,' broke in Wainwright, 'and so he did. But the emeralds weren't in it. They were in my pocket!'

17

Jukes Has an Idea

Under the astonished gaze of Fordyce and the inspector, Wainwright plunged his hand into his trouser pocket, and withdrew it full of the glittering green stones.

'I guessed something might happen directly the lights went out,' he said, 'and so I took the precaution of sweeping these off the table into my pocket. I put the base back on the White Queen, and hoped that our friend in his eagerness wouldn't investigate what he was getting too closely.'

'I never saw you do it,' declared John. 'I thought he'd got away with the stones.'

'So did he,' murmured Wainwright, and smiled.

'Well, sir,' said Jukes heavily. 'I must congratulate you on a very clever trick. You say this man who held you up spoke to you? Did either of you recognise his voice?'

Wainwright shook his head, and slipped the emeralds back into his pocket.

'No,' he answered. 'He was speaking in a high pitched squeaky voice, obviously disguised.'

John confirmed this, and the inspector frowned.

'Well,' he said, 'when I came up here tonight, I thought I'd got the case more or less clear, but I don't mind admitting that this new development doesn't fit in with my theory.'

He sighed heavily.

'What was your theory?' asked John interestedly.

The inspector cleared his throat, and looked from John to Wainwright and back again, to John.

'Well, sir,' he said speaking slowly and distinctly as though he were considering every word, 'this afternoon after Mr. Elford had identified the body, and told me that it was 'Shiner' Talbot, I got through to the Yard for further information. They told me all about the emerald robbery, and I asked them for any other details of Talbot's past life that were known. About an hour ago they rang me up at the station, and told me they were sending a man down to enquire into Inspector Blackwood's murder, Superintendent Hanford.'

'Hanford?' exclaimed a voice from the door, and they looked round quickly to see Frank Elford standing on the threshold.

He had come across from the drawing room and been in time to hear the latter part of what Jukes was saying.

'Do you know him, sir?' asked the inspector.

'Very well,' Frank came into the room, and closed the door behind him. 'When is he coming?'

'In the morning,' answered Jukes, and then after a momentary pause he continued: 'At the same time they told me something else, and it was this information that brought me up here tonight.'

'What did they tell you?' asked John.

'They asked me,' answered Jukes looking at him steadily, 'if anything had been seen or heard of Talbot's wife.'

'Talbot's wife?' echoed Elford.

The inspector nodded ponderously.

'Yes, sir,' he said. 'It appears he was married to a girl named Lydia Holland, about three years before the Bond Street job. She was a crook too; had been convicted twice for theft although she wasn't more than eighteen at the time.'

He paused again, and Wainwright said quickly: 'Why did Scotland Yard think that anything might have been seen of her here?'

'They say that she and Talbot always worked together,' replied the inspector. 'It was believed that she went abroad soon after he was sentenced because they lost trace of her.'

'She may be still be abroad,' put in Fordyce. 'Anyway I don't see how she can be connected with this affair.'

Jukes smiled.

'I'm coming to that, sir,' he said. 'When I heard about this woman I was naturally interested, and I got the Yard to give me a detailed description of her, and — '

He stopped and looked from one to the other.

'Well?' said John impatiently, 'Go on!'

'Well, sir,' said the inspector. 'It's my opinion that she's a member of your household.'

John stared at him in amazement.

'My household!' he exclaimed. 'Nonsense! Who could it be?'

'The description they gave me of Lydia Talbot,' said Jukes, rolling the words out slowly, as though he were enjoying the sensation he was creating, 'applies exactly to your housemaid, Anne Barton.'

'Anne!' cried the astonished John, 'Rubbish!'

The inspector's heavy face darkened slightly. He was obviously annoyed at this reception to his carefully exploded bombshell.

'I don't think you'll say that, sir,' he retorted, 'when you've heard all I've got to say. We're pretty certain that whoever the unknown man in the mask is he's got a confederate inside the house. Someone left the library window open that night when Talbot was murdered, and if Anne is Lydia Talbot then I don't think we need look any further.'

'I don't quite understand you,' said

Elford frowning. 'If she's working in collusion with this unknown man, it must have been against her husband, because it was he who murdered Talbot.'

Jukes looked at him queerly.

'I see,' he said, raising his heavy eyebrows. 'You think that, eh?'

'Don't you?' snapped the reporter.

'No, sir, I do not,' replied Jukes. 'I've got a theory to account for the murder of Talbot, and Blackwood, and I don't think either of them was killed by the man outside.'

'Let us hear this remarkable idea of yours, Inspector,' said Wainwright coolly as Jukes stopped to watch the effect of his words.

The inspector drew a deep breath and moistened his lips.

'I'll tell you how I've worked it out,' he said. 'Listen. Talbot, the moment he was released from prison, came here after those emeralds — '

'How did he know they were in the house?' interrupted Wainwright, and Jukes looked a little disconcerted.

'I'm not quite clear on that point, sir,' he admitted, 'but for the sake of my theory we'll assume that he did know. He probably expected to find the house empty, and when he discovered that Mr. Fordyce had just moved in, it upset his plans. He arranged, however, for his wife to obtain a situation as housemaid with the aid of faked references, and later, on her recommendation, got himself the job as chauffeur under the name of Gore. Do you agree with me, sir?'

'Yes, so far,' said Wainwright nodding.

'I see, so far,' said Jukes. 'Well, I'll go farther. Having succeeded in getting into the house he began, with the assistance of his wife, to search for the stones, but without finding a trace of them.'

'How about the unknown man in the mask?' asked Fordyce.

'One moment, sir,' protested Jukes, a little annoyed at being interrupted. 'I haven't finished yet, I'm coming to him now. This man, Talbot, had been imprisoned for nearly five years and his wife, well, she's pretty and she's young and human nature is human nature,' he smiled a little unpleasantly, 'suppose during her husband's absence,' he went on, 'she had formed another attachment? And supposing she told this lover of hers about the emeralds, and they decided to wait until Talbot had found them and then secure them for themselves. What is more natural than that he should come here and lurk about the grounds ready to receive the news from Mrs. Talbot directly the stones were found.'

'But it was Anne herself,' protested Wainwright, 'who was the first to draw attention to him. She would hardly do that if — '

'No, sir, it wasn't,' broke in Jukes triumphantly. 'It was the kitchen maid who saw him first. Isn't that right, sir?'

He appealed to John and the latter nodded.

'Quite right,' he said, 'but otherwise I think you're talking a lot of nonsense. If you don't think that this man whoever he is, had anything to do with the murders, whom do you suspect?'

'Mrs. Talbot!' answered Jukes.

'Bunk!' exclaimed Elford. 'Why should she kill her husband?'

'I'll tell you,' grunted the inspector,

his face a little flushed with annoyance, 'because he found out that she was carrying on with this other man.'

'She couldn't have done it,' said Wainwright shaking his head decisively. 'When Talbot was killed, Anne was upstairs preparing a room for me.'

'I know she was,' retorted the inspector, 'and that doesn't prove anything. I've thought of all that. Perhaps you've forgotten the fire escape which leads from all the rooms on the second floor to the ground.'

Wainwright was taken aback.

'I had,' he admitted.

'I hadn't,' said Jukes complacently. 'But for that my theory would fall to the ground.' He leaned forward and looked at them impressively. 'I believe this is what happened,' he continued choosing his words carefully. 'Talbot discovered what was going on, and on the night of his murder — returning with the parcel of books from Tor Bridge — saw this unknown man hanging about Beech Drive and tackled him. Mrs. Talbot from the window of Mr. Wainwright's room saw what was happening — she could easily, that part of the drive where the car stopped is visible from there — she saw that the two men were quarrelling, and climbed down the fire escape with the intention of interfering. By the time she reached the ground her husband was approaching the house, followed by her lover. Talbot put the parcel on the steps, and turned to continue his argument with the other man. Probably he pulled a knife from his pocket and attacked him. His wife wrenched the weapon from his hand and stabbed him. He had enough strength to stagger to the front door, but failing to get an answer to his second knock, started to crawl round to the other entrance; found the library window open, and collapsing against it, fell into the room. In the meanwhile his wife hurried her lover away, and slipped back up the fire escape. How's that?'

If he expected to receive any congratulations on this ingenious reconstruction, he was disappointed, for the only comment was made by Wainwright.

'It doesn't account for Blackwood's death,' he said. 'Perhaps you can explain that.'

'I think I can, sir,' answered Jukes. 'He

was at the railway station at Tor Bridge when Talbot called for the parcel, and he recognised him. Making enquiries he found that he was working at Raven House, and decided to call and warn Mr. Fordyce of the character of the man he had in his employ.'

'Is this more theory?' asked John disparagingly.

'No, sir, it's fact!' retorted Jukes. 'I was at the railway station this afternoon and got a signed statement from a porter to that effect. My idea is that Blackwood was just coming up the drive at the time Talbot was killed, and was a witness of what took place. They had to kill him, too, for the sake of their necks.'

There was a silence after he finished speaking, broken at last by Wainwright.

'Inspector Jukes,' he said slowly, 'you are considerably cleverer than I imagined.'

'Thank you, sir,' said the gratified inspector.

'After all,' remarked Elford, 'It's only surmise, and rests entirely on the fact that Anne is Mrs. Talbot. If you've made a mistake — well your theory comes to grief, doesn't it?'

Jukes nodded.

'It does,' he agreed, 'but it's easily proved. If you will ring for Anne now, Mr. Fordyce, we'll put it to the test.'

18

Anne

Anne came, subdued and respectful. She closed the door behind her, and stood on the threshold looking from one to the other enquiringly.

'Inspector Jukes has something to say to you, Anne,' said John a little uncomfortably.

She inclined her head without speaking, and the inspector stared at her for a few moments before he began.

'Your name is Anne Barton, isn't it?' he said at last.

'Yes, sir.' Her voice was low and clear and perfectly steady.

'Are you sure?' he went on.

The slightest trace of surprise showed for an instant in her face.

'Of course,' she answered.

He moved a few steps towards her.

'I was wondering if it wasn't — Lydia,' he said sharply.

She gave an almost imperceptible start, and he went on quickly:

'You're certain it's not Lydia — Lydia Talbot?'

His little pig-like eyes were fixed on her steadily, but she returned his gaze without flinching.

'I ought to know my own name, sir,' she said quietly.

'You ought,' he snapped, 'but it may have slipped your memory — in five years.'

Her thinly pencilled brows moved upwards slightly.

'Five years?' she repeated questioningly.

'Yes.' He thrust out his chin aggressively towards her. 'I don't suppose you've used it since your husband was sentenced. It wasn't a name to be proud of, was it?'

'I — ' she moistened her lips. 'I don't understand what you mean,' she said in a low voice.

'Oh, you don't, eh?' growled Jukes. 'Well I'll tell you. The man who was murdered here last night was Simon Talbot, a jewel thief, your husband!'

He waited for her to reply, but she remained silent, and now she had dropped her eyes and was looking on the floor.

'Answer my question!' he thundered.

'You didn't ask me a question,' she said calmly raising her head. 'You made a statement!'

'You can't get out of it that way,' he sneered. 'Was Simon Talbot your husband?'

'I am not married,' she answered, and Jukes made an impatient gesture.

'I know you're not now,' he retorted. 'But you were until last night.'

Again she was silent, and he went on loudly:

'Stop hiding up, will you, and let's have the truth!'

'I never had a husband,' she said in a voice that was barely audible. 'You've made a mistake — '

'I'm not going to argue about that,' he interrupted. 'I'll put it another way. Shall we say you were *known* as Mrs. Talbot?'

A slight flush crept into her pale cheeks, and her eyes glittered.

'You've no right to say that!' she flashed quickly.

'I see, I've no right, eh?' he smiled unpleasantly. 'Perhaps it was too near the truth. Perhaps you'd prefer it if I called you Lydia Holland?'

'I'd prefer it if you didn't speak to me at all!' she snapped.

'I daresay you would,' he answered, 'but you can't get out of it. It's no good trying to bluff with me, I've had a full description of you from Scotland Yard, and you're the woman who was generally supposed to be Mrs. Talbot. I don't care whether you were married or not — I don't expect you were. Crooks of Talbot's type hate anything legal; probably there are scores of Mrs. Talbots — '

'You liar!' she cried furiously. 'That's not true, I — '

He crossed quickly over to her side.

'Then what is the truth?' he said, his face a few inches from hers. 'Come on, out with it! You *are* Lydia Talbot!'

She shrank away from him, and then recovering herself, she said:

'Well supposing I am? You've got

210

nothing against me because of that.'

'Oh, haven't I?' he snapped harshly. 'What are you doing here, pretending to be a maid in another name?'

'Earning my living!' she retorted. 'There's no law against that, is there?'

'No,' answered Jukes. 'But there's a law against — murder!'

The colour left her face, draining away until she was white to the lips, and her eyes went misty with fear. For a moment she swayed, and Elford thinking she was going to fall, sprang forward. But before he could reach her she had recovered herself.

'What do you mean, murder?' she asked huskily.

'Simon Talbot was murdered,' said Jukes meaningfully, 'and you know who killed him.'

'I?' she laughed, a little shrill high- pitched laugh that jarred the nerves of the listeners. 'God, I wish I did! If I knew the man who'd done that, I'd never leave him until — I'd served him the same way.'

'Perhaps it wasn't a man at all?' suggested the inspector sternly.

'What do you mean?' she asked, and she was either a wonderful actress or the surprised expression on her face was genuine.

'I believe that you killed your husband!' he snapped watching her intently.

The surprise on her face changed to incredulity, and her lips parted soundlessly as she stared at him in sheer amazement.

'You believe — I — killed — Sim?' she said jerkily. 'You're mad! Why should I kill him? Why should I kill the only human being I ever loved, or whoever loved me?'

'Because,' said Jukes, dropping his voice impressively, 'of the man who is always hanging round this house.'

He stopped, but the expression of his eyes told her what he meant, and the blood came flaming back into her cheeks.

'You beast!' she cried hoarsely. 'You foul-minded beast! So that's what you think, do you?'

'Do you deny it?' he asked sharply.

'Yes, of course I do,' she answered vehemently. 'I don't know who he is any more than you do, except that he's a murderer! Lover!' She laughed again scornfully. 'I only had one lover, and he was lover, husband, child, everything!'

'And a thief,' sneered Jukes.

'Yes, and a thief,' she retorted. The tears welled up into her eyes, but she choked them back. 'But if he'd got away with those emeralds, he'd have more than earned them, with the time he spent working in the stone quarries on the 'Moor'. And the hours of solitude in a stone cell. Earned them with five years of unadulterated hell . . . '

'That sounds fine,' said the inspector as she stopped breathless, 'but what proof can you give me that you didn't kill Talbot?'

'What proofs have you that I did?' she snapped back.

'None, at the moment,' he said, 'but I'm going to do my best to find some. Where's your room?'

She told him, and he moved past her to the door.

'I'm going to search it,' he said with his hand on the handle, and she swung round towards him.

'Have you got a warrant?' she asked.

He shook his head, and the expression on his face was unpleasant.

'No, but I'll risk that,' he answered. 'You stay here until I come back.' He glanced across at John. 'I rely on you, Mr. Fordyce, to see that she doesn't get away,' he snapped, and pulling open the door he went out, slamming it behind him.

'H'm!' remarked Wainwright. 'An energetic officer, Jukes. He should go far.'

'The farther the better, I should think,' grunted Elford. 'What an unpleasant brute!'

Wainwright nodded slowly.

'Yes, he's an acquired taste, like spinach,' he said, 'but thorough, very thorough.' He turned towards Anne. 'So you are really Lydia Talbot, eh?' he asked kindly.

She was trembling violently. The control that she had put upon her nerves had broken, and going over to her, John led her to a chair and sat her down. Wainwright repeated his question, and she nodded.

'Yes, it was no good denying it,' she

said brokenly. 'I guessed he'd search my room, and my marriage certificate is in my trunk.'

'Have you any idea who killed your husband?' asked Wainwright, and again she shook her head.

'No,' she answered. 'I told Inspector Jukes the truth. I wish I had.'

The tears were running down her cheeks unchecked, and she searched in the pocket of her apron for a handkerchief.

'Why did you open that window in the library last night?' said Wainwright, and her eyes widened with surprise.

'I never opened any window,' she answered, and he believed her.

'Do you know anything at all about this affair?' he went on. 'Beyond the emeralds, I mean? Any reason why Talbot should have been killed?'

'No, I know nothing,' she declared. 'I swear to you that I know nothing.'

There was a momentary silence. She was still searching for a non-existent handkerchief, and seeing her dilemma John took a clean one from the breast pocket of his jacket and handed it to her. She thanked him gratefully, and dabbed at her eyes.

'Tell me,' he said presently, 'how did these emeralds get in the house?'

She looked up at him a little startled.

'Must I answer that?' she asked.

'You'll have to sooner or later,' said Wainwright gently, 'so you might as well tell us now.'

She hesitated, and then making up her mind, she said in a low voice:

'They were brought here by your uncle, William Grant.'

'How did they come into his possession?' asked Fordyce.

'Well you see, sir,' she moved uncomfortably, 'when Sim did the job at Lowenstein and Marks, he took the emeralds to your uncle for disposal.'

'You mean,' explained John, 'that my uncle was a fence?'

She nodded.

'Yes,' she answered. 'Sim used to put all his business through Grant. He had a little office in Upper Thames Street; all the big jewel thieves knew him. But he wouldn't do anything with the emeralds, because he said they would be too easily traced. And if they were cut, it would ruin their value. He suggested holding them up until the affair had blown over.'

'I see,' said Wainwright, 'and in the meantime Talbot was arrested.'

'Yes,' she replied.

John opened his lips to ask a question, but before he could get the words out the door was thrown open and Jukes entered. His heavy face was smiling and triumphant.

'Now, Lydia Talbot, Holland or whatever you call yourself,' he cried, coming over and confronting her, 'explain *that* away!'

He took his hand from behind his back, and held it out almost under her nose. In the palm lay a long-bladed knife, and the shining steel was crusted with dried blood!

19

In the Night

Anne shrank away from the horrible thing with a little gasp of terror.

'What is it?' muttered John.

'It's the knife that killed Talbot and Blackwood,' answered the inspector grimly. 'I found it in her trunk concealed amongst some clothing.'

'I've never seen it before,' whispered Anne her eyes fixed on it with a fascinated stare, 'I swear to you I've never seen it before!'

'You tell that to the judge!' snapped Jukes, 'maybe he'll believe you, and maybe he won't!'

With an effort she tore her eyes from the weapon and looked up at him.

'The judge?' she repeated fearfully.

He nodded.

'Yes, I'm going to arrest you for wilful murder,' he said sternly, and Wainwright lounged forward.

'I don't think I should do that, Inspector, if I were you,' he said gently.

Jukes swung round on him angrily.

'I'll trouble you not to interfere, sir!' he snapped.

'I'm only interfering for your own good,' said Wainwright. 'If you arrest this girl, you'll get yourself into trouble.'

'Oh, shall I?' sneered the inspector. 'Well, I'll risk that! This is proof enough for me.'

He tapped the knife.

'It's proof enough for me, too,' said Wainwright; 'conclusive proof that Anne is not guilty.'

They looked at him in astonishment.

'What do you mean?' asked the inspector frowning.

'Merely this,' answered Wainwright, taking his cigarette case from his pocket and helping himself to a cigarette. 'I searched her room and her luggage thoroughly this afternoon. There was no knife there then.'

Anne's eyes widened with amazement.

'You — then you must have known that

I was — ' Her voice trailed away incoherently.

Wainwright nodded coolly and lit his cigarette.

'That you were Mrs. Talbot?' he said. 'Yes, I knew that.'

'Oh, you knew that, did you?' said Jukes, his face red with anger. 'Then why didn't you tell me at once?'

'I thought it better to let you find out for yourself,' answered Wainwright, blowing out a cloud of smoke.

'I should have been told,' said the inspector gruffly. 'Concealing evidence likely to help the police is an offence, sir, a very serious offence!'

'I believe it is,' murmured Wainwright disinterestedly.

'May I ask,' Jukes went on, 'what led you to search this woman's luggage?'

'Put it down to sheer vulgar curiosity,' was the bland reply. 'Anyway, it was a very good job I did, otherwise I shouldn't be in the position to stop you making a fool of yourself.'

Jukes pursed his lips and his brows drew together over his small eyes.

'If she didn't hide this knife in her trunk,' he demanded, 'who did?'

'Obviously someone who wanted to throw suspicion on her,' answered Wainwright.

Jukes looked at him with narrowed eyes, and he went on quickly:

'It wasn't me, you needn't get that idea into your head. I couldn't have committed either of the crimes.'

'H'm!' snorted the inspector. 'Well, your testimony may be very interesting, but it's not going to stop me arresting this woman on suspicion.'

'You must do as you think best,' said Wainwright seriously, 'but I warn you, you'll get into serious trouble if you do. For one thing you haven't got a warrant, and for another, you haven't sufficient proof.'

'She's a crook,' grunted Jukes stubbornly.

'She may be,' retorted Wainwright, 'but that doesn't make her a murderess! Take my advice, Inspector, and wait until Superintendent Hanford arrives in the morning.'

'When he does arrive,' said Jules viciously, 'I shall have something to say to him about people interfering with the police in the execution of their duty!'

Wainwright smiled.

'Don't be silly, Inspector,' he said sweetly. 'You'll thank me later on for preventing you making a serious mistake.'

The inspector didn't look like thanking anybody at that moment. His face was dark with anger, and it was only by an effort that he succeeded in controlling his temper.

'I shan't forget to mention your attitude, Mr. Wainwright, when I make my report,' he said, stiffly, 'but at the moment I will leave things as they are. You understand, though, that if this woman leaves the house,' he looked across at John Fordyce, 'you will be held responsible, Mr. Fordyce?'

'We understand that,' said Wainwright before John could answer, 'and I can promise you that she won't leave the house until after Superintendent Hanford has given her permission.'

'Very well,' said the inspector, 'then I

might as well be getting back to the station.'

He wrapped the knife up carefully in his handkerchief, and put it away in his inside breast pocket. His hand was on the knob of the door when he remembered something, and turned back.

'I'd better take those emeralds with me,' he said.

'I think they'll be safer here,' said Wainwright shaking his head. 'You've a long distance to go to the police station, and in all probability the masked man is still hanging about somewhere.'

Jukes appeared to be about to protest, evidently changed his mind and shrugged his shoulders.

'Well, as long as you're willing to accept the responsibility, I don't mind,' he said ungraciously. 'Have you got a safe or anything you can keep them in?'

He addressed the last remark to Fordyce, and John shook his head.

'I don't suppose there'll be any further attempt to get them tonight,' remarked Wainwright, 'and tomorrow they can be handed over to Superintendent Hanford.'

He looked about the room, and chuckled softly. 'In the meantime I should think that would be as safe as anywhere.' He crossed over to the fireplace and opened the front of the clock on the mantelpiece. 'Yes, there's plenty of room,' he said, 'and that's about the last place one would expect to find two hundred thousand pounds' worth of emeralds.'

'Well, it's your responsibility,' grunted Jukes. 'Good night, Mr. Fordyce. I shall be along with the Superintendent first thing in the morning. Keep an eye on Mrs. Talbot, he'll want her, and it's going to be unpleasant for a lot of people if she isn't there!'

He glared aggressively at Wainwright, nodded curtly to Elford and, pulling open the door, went out. A moment later they heard the front door slam and the sound of his retreating footsteps crunching on the gravel.

'Do you — do you want me any more?' asked Anne breaking the silence that followed the inspector's departure.

John shook his head, and she rose to her feet, and went over to the door. On the threshold she paused.

'I suppose I ought to thank you, sir,' she said looking at Wainwright, 'and I do, but I can't think of how to say it.'

'Then don't,' he answered good humouredly and with a faint smile she went out.

'I'm surprised Jukes didn't insist on arresting her,' remarked Elford when she had gone.

'I think he realised himself that it would be a mistake,' answered Wainwright. 'Have you got a small box of any sort, John?'

Fordyce went over to the desk and made a search.

'Is this any good?' he asked presently holding out a small carton of paper clips.

'The very thing,' said his friend, and John emptied the clips into a drawer and handed him the box. 'Now I want a piece of paper and some string,' he said, as he began taking the emeralds from his pocket and dropping them into the box.

When this was forthcoming, and he had satisfied himself that he hadn't overlooked any of the stones, he made up a neat package which he stowed away in the lower part of the clock case.

'And that's that,' he said.

'Do you think they'll be safe there?' asked John a little anxiously.

'As safe there as anywhere,' answered Wainwright, and at that moment the door opened and Eustace came in.

He seemed a little surprised to see them, and stood for a moment uncertainly on the threshold.

'Hello,' said John, 'What do you want?'

'I came to see if there was any paper,' answered Eustace, 'I'm writing a poem and I've used up all my supply. Could you let me have a little?'

John nodded towards the desk.

'You'll find plenty there,' he said, 'in the left hand drawer.'

Eustace thanked him politely, and walked delicately over to the desk.

'Where have you been all the evening?' asked Wainwright abruptly and the youthful poet looked round.

'Upstairs in my room,' he said, and a momentary expression of uneasiness crossed his face. 'Why?'

'I only wanted to know,' replied Wainwright.

'You see,' Eustace went on hesitantly, 'I wanted to write this little thing about the rain, and I must say I've caught the atmosphere wonderfully. I don't want you to say anything to Mater about it but — ' He paused and his sallow face flushed.

'But what?' said John. 'What is it you don't want us to tell your mother?'

'Well the fact is,' Eustace went on confidentially, 'I've lighted a little fire, and she'd be awfully cross if she knew. She's very funny about things at times, you know.'

Wainwright laughed.

'You needn't worry, we shan't tell her,' he said, and with a little sigh of relief Eustace turned his attention to the desk.

'Well, we've got a little farther,' said Elford, 'but not much. I wonder who opened the library window last night, if it wasn't Anne.'

'I think it must have been,' said John. 'Probably she did do it and didn't like to admit it.'

'I don't know,' muttered Wainwright. 'I don't think she was lying.'

'She wasn't, if you mean this window,'

said Eustace looking round, several sheets of writing paper in his hand. 'I opened it!'

'You did, eh?' said Wainwright. 'Why?'

'Well, it was last night that I first got the idea for this little poem of mine,' explained Eustace. 'I wanted to absorb the right atmosphere. I think that's always so important, don't you? So I came in here and stood for a little while at the open window, I remembered afterwards that I'd forgotten to shut it.'

'Why didn't you tell us this before?' demanded John roughly, and Eustace looked at him in hurt surprise.

'Well really, no one asked me,' he replied.

Wainwright questioned him closely concerning the time, but he could not remember. He had not thought it very important, and apparently did not think so now, for he was rather astonished at their persistence. Eventually they let him go and he hurried away clasping his blank sheets of paper.

Dinner was very late that night, and none of them with the exception of Peggy and Georgina, who had already changed, troubled to dress. The conversation through-out the meal centred on the exciting events of the evening, and the discussion contin-ued afterwards in the drawing room where they had their coffee. Peggy was surprised to learn the real identity of Anne, but if Georgina felt any astonishment she was very clever at concealing the fact. Mid-night came before they realised how quickly the time had passed, and as they broke up to go to their various rooms, Wainwright called Elford to one side.

'Come to my room in ten minutes,' he whispered. 'I want to talk to you.'

The reporter nodded, and with a cheery good night to John went slowly up the stairs. Wainwright followed him almost immediately, leaving Fordyce to put the lights out and lock up.

By one o'clock the house was in darkness, and although the majority of its inmates were in bed and asleep, there were some who remained wakeful.

Outside the night was dark and gusty. A cold wind blew over the wide expanse of the moor, whistling through the leafless branches of the gaunt trees, and rustling the ivy as it sighed round the house. There was no moon, for a heavy wrack of rain clouds covered the sky. In the darkness of the shrubbery on the right of Beech Drive, a darker patch of shadow moved stealthily towards the house, and pausing some fifty yards away, watched expectantly as the lights went out one by one. As the last one vanished, the black clad figure crept cautiously forward until it merged with the dark bulk of the building . . .

In her little room on the top floor, Anne sat on the side of her bed fully dressed and stared into vacancy. She had sat thus for a long time. Across the small window she had pinned a blanket so that no ray of light from the flickering candle that burned on the table by her side could be seen from without. She had made up her mind what she was going to do, it was the only thing to be done under the circumstances. Presently she glanced at her watch, and rising to her feet began noiselessly to set about her preparations. From a cupboard in one corner she brought out a suitcase, and laying this open on the bed, she began to pack it with such essentials from her trunk as it was necessary for her to take. A great deal of her possessions she would have to leave behind, for she could not burden herself with more than one small case. The few things she possessed that were of sentimental value, she would take, and the others she could replace later. She finished packing the suitcase, closed it and locked it and straightening up went over to the door, and fetched her coat, which hung on a hook behind it. It was a serviceable coat of dark tweed, plain and inconspicuous, and she wanted to be as inconspicuous as possible. She put it on, and then pulled a small hat over her auburn hair. Her face was powderless and devoid of make-up, and this she remedied in front of the little mirror on her dressing table.

Standing in the centre of the room she looked round her quickly to make sure she had forgotten nothing that was essential. She had almost decided that she had not when she suddenly remembered, and going over to the tiny fireplace, felt with her gloved hand up the chimney. There was a ledge just behind the register, and from this she brought forth a small revolver.

It had been given to her some years previously by her husband, and she had almost forgotten it. She dusted the soot off it carefully with a face towel, and examined the mechanism to see that it was working. It was fully loaded, and as she spun the cylinder the brass ends of the cartridges glinted wickedly in the light of the candle.

She dropped it into her pocket and looked at her watch again. It was a quarter to two. She concluded that the rest of the household had had ample time to get to sleep, and picking up her suitcase she blew out the candle, and going over to the door unlocked it. Standing in the narrow passageway outside, she listened carefully.

The house was very silent, no sound of shuffling footsteps, and muffled tapping reached her ears now, and as the thought passed quickly through her mind, her eyes moistened. The man who had made those would never make another sound. She moved cautiously along to the stairs, and began to creep down. She made no sound, being well acquainted with the treads that were solid and those that creaked. She reached the lower landing, and here she paused again.

From somewhere along a corridor to her right came a muffled snore, but otherwise the silence was unbroken. She went on, a ghostly figure in that silent house, until she reached the hall, pitch black and filled with the monotonous ticking of the big grandfather clock.

Setting down her suitcase near the front door, she felt her way to the library. On the threshold she hesitated for a second, her hand going up to the light switch. Should she risk it and put the lights on? She decided not to, she knew exactly where the emeralds were, and it would be better not to chance the light being seen. Leaving the door open, she made her way over to the fireplace, and reaching up, opened the front of the clock. Feeling about in the interior of the case, her fingers closed on the little packet, and she gave a sigh of thankfulness. As she withdrew it, she heard a faint sound behind her and swung round.

'If you move or scream, I'll kill you!' whispered a high-pitched squeaky voice, and she knew that she was face to face with the man who had killed her husband!

20

Surprise!

She held her breath, straining her eyes to pierce the darkness, but she could see nothing. In the silence that followed that horrible menacing voice, she could hear her own quickly beating heart, and the soft breathing of the man in the room.

'You thought you'd double cross me, eh?' he went on in a sibilant whisper. 'You fool! I guessed you'd try something like this.'

'Who are you?' she breathed.

He chuckled softly.

'As long as you don't know that, you're safe,' he answered. 'Talbot and Blackwood knew — and they died!'

'You damned swine!' she said between her teeth. 'You killed Sim!'

She made a movement with her hand towards her coat pocket, but before she could reach it, a ray of light from a torch leaped out of the darkness, and focussed on her.

'Keep still!' hissed the voice warningly. 'Don't try and find that pistol you've got in your pocket, or I'll send you to hell to join your husband! Yes, I killed Talbot!'

She stood motionless, blinking in the strong light.

'Why did you kill him?' she asked. 'What harm had he ever done you?'

'He recognised me that night in the drive,' he answered. 'If he'd only listened to reason he might have been alive now. I was willing to give him a share in the emeralds, but he only laughed at me. He was too greedy. While we were talking the mask slipped, and he recognised me. I had to kill him after that for my own safety. I crept up behind him after he thought I'd gone, and stabbed him as he put the parcel down on the step.'

'You devil!' she whispered hoarsely. 'I'd give something to know who you are.'

He laughed, a little thin sneering laugh.

'Do you think I'd tell you all this, if I thought you'd ever find out?' he said.

'I will find out!' she retorted. 'It may

take me years, but I'll get you, for what you did to Sim!'

'You won't have a chance,' he answered. 'It'll take someone cleverer than you to find me, once I leave here.'

'Do you think you'll get away?' she said. 'You're a fool if you do! One of the cleverest men at the Yard's coming here tomorrow.'

'Blackwood was clever too,' he interrupted, 'but it didn't help him much!'

'Why did you kill him?' she asked.

She was talking for the sake of gaining time, her brain working rapidly to try and discover some means of getting the better of this man who had surprised her at the moment when she had almost made her getaway.

'I had to,' he answered, 'he came up the drive just after I'd finished Talbot and nearly caught me. But I'm wasting time. Give me those emeralds!'

'If only you hadn't got that pistol,' she muttered.

'But I have,' he snapped, 'and that makes all the difference! Come on, give me that packet!'

'All right, take it,' she said shrugging her shoulders, and made a movement as though to hold it out to him, and then as he moved forward, she suddenly flung it with all her force at the place where she judged his face would be. It evidently hit him, for she heard a muttered oath, and the torch dropped from his hand. It didn't go out, and darting to it she picked it up. Turning its light on the man who had by now recovered from his momentary surprise, she was in time to see him raise the pistol that he held. But she had drawn her own from her pocket, and before his finger could tighten on the trigger she brought the butt of the little weapon down on his wrist. He gave a squeak of pain, and the automatic dropped from his fingers. She kicked it out of the way and covered him with her own revolver.

'Now it's my turn!' she hissed. 'Get over there against the wall! I'm going to see who you are!'

'Damn you!' he muttered, his eyes glistening through the slits in the mask that covered his face. 'You — '

'Don't talk, move!' she snapped; and after a second's hesitation he backed slowly towards the wall.

She followed him, the pistol in her hand unwavering.

'Now,' she said, 'take off that mask!'

He made no movement, and she made a menacing gesture with the muzzle of the weapon.

'Take it off!' she went on. 'I want to see the face of the man who killed Sim!'

Slowly his gloved hands went up until they reached the strip of black silk, and then with a quick movement he tore it from his face.

'My God! You!' she gasped, and she was so startled at the revelation, that she momentarily lowered the pistol she held.

He took instant advantage of her surprise. Like lightning his right hand darted down and gripped her wrist. He gave it a quick savage twist, and the pistol fell to the floor as she uttered a cry of pain.

'You'll carry your knowledge to the grave!' he said harshly, and his hands went up and gripped her by the throat.

She gave a muffled scream, and the

torch went out as he bore her backwards to the floor. The grip on her throat tightened, and the blood began to pound in her temples. In the darkness before her eyes splashes of red light leaped and danced, and whirled, and then dimly she heard a voice shouting, and the clasp on her throat relaxed.

The man who was strangling her leaped to his feet, as the lights in the library came on in a blinding glare and made a dash for the french window.

'Hold him, Elford!' cried Wainwright's voice. 'Don't let him get away.' And as Anne scrambled to her feet she saw him standing in the open doorway, his hand on the light switch.

Frank Elford reached the man just as he was pulling at the hasp of the windows, and throwing his arm around him dragged him back. He fought furiously, kicking and struggling, and muttering a string of foul oaths. With a crash they both fell to the floor, and Wainwright hurried forward to the assistance of the reporter. Anne picked up her revolver, and leaning shakily back against the wall watched the struggling figures. The man was as strong as an ox, and he succeeded in throwing off Elford, but before he could get to his feet, Wainwright had flung himself upon him. They rolled over and over and in the midst of the struggle, John Fordyce suddenly appeared at the library door, a dressing gown over his pyjamas, and his hair awry. He stared in surprise at the fighting men, and then he saw Anne.

'Anne!' he exclaimed. 'What are you doing here? What's happening?'

'Come here, Fordyce, will you?' panted Wainwright before Anne could reply.

John joined the struggling group, and with his assistance they succeeded in overpowering the unknown and dragging him to his feet.

'Twist his arm behind his back, Elford,' muttered Wainwright. 'Now let's have a look at you!'

The man's head was sunk on his chest, and gripping him under the chin Wainwright jerked it up.

'My God!' exclaimed John, as the light fell full on the other's distorted face. 'Jukes!'

'I thought so,' said Wainwright.

'But what does it mean?' muttered John.

'It means that we've caught the great unknown,' answered his friend. 'The man who killed Talbot and poor Blackwood.'

'There must be some mistake.' John rubbed his forehead perplexedly. 'It can't be Jukes.'

'There's no mistake,' said Wainwright. 'He gave himself away to Anne a few seconds ago. Elford and I overheard him.'

'It seems incredible,' muttered John, half disbelievingly.

'I daresay it does,' said Wainwright, 'but it's true. He's been waiting for years for the chance of laying his hands on those emeralds. He knew all about the Bond Street robbery, but he didn't know what had happened to the stones until Talbot arrived at Raven House. Then he was certain they were hidden here. He hoped to scare you away by throwing that warning through the window, but that little plan went astray. Didn't it — Rosher?'

Jukes started and his angry eyes glared murder at the man before him.

'God!' he muttered. 'Do you know that?'

'I know everything,' answered Wainwright

immodestly. 'You didn't think I knew that, did you? You didn't think that anyone knew that Rosher, the fence, and Inspector Jukes, the rural policeman, were one and the same. You thought you'd been too clever, didn't you? And so you had — up to a point. Scotland Yard never even suspected it until three months ago, when they pulled in Duke Soames for the Knightsbridge robbery, and he swore he'd sold Lady Conway's pearls to Rosher. The transaction took place at four cross roads, a mile outside Princetown, and the man who bought the pearls from Soames was masked and came in a car. That was the only description that Soames could give, with the exception that he noticed that the man was wearing a gold signet ring on the little finger of his left hand. It had a green shield.' Wainwright stopped and learning forward pulled off the black glove from Jukes' left hand. 'You're still wearing that ring, Rosher!'

The trapped man glanced down at his finger.

'If I'd thought for a moment that you knew,' he snarled, 'I'd — '

'Have done the hat trick, eh?' broke in Wainwright pleasantly. 'Well, that wouldn't have helped you. I telephoned all I suspected to Hanford at Scotland Yard this afternoon.'

'Hanford,' muttered Jukes. His eyes were searching the floor, and suddenly a little gleam crept into them as they lighted on the automatic pistol, which Anne had struck from his hand previously.

'Yes,' continued Wainwright, 'and I asked them to telephone you and say that they were sending a man down in the morning to investigate Blackwood's death. I wanted to force your hand and I did! You knew that tonight was your last chance — that the emeralds would be handed over to Hanford in the morning, and you made your bid. You wouldn't have got much, though, if you had succeeded in getting away with that packet. It only contains coal! I substituted it for the real packet earlier, guessing that some attempt like this would be made.'

'You clever devil!' said the inspector hoarsely.

'Thanks for the compliment,' said

Wainwright. 'It frightened you when you knew Hanford was coming, didn't it? So much so that to avoid any chance of your being suspected, you tried all you could to fasten the crime on to Mrs. Talbot, and — '

'Look out!' cried Elford, for Jukes with a sudden and unexpected movement had wrenched himself free, and stooping quickly snatched up the automatic that lay a few yards from his feet.

'You may have caught me,' he snarled, backing towards the windows, 'but you can't hold me!'

He covered them with the weapon, his little eyes narrowed almost to pinpoints.

'I've still got a chance and I'm going to take it! But before I go, Wainwright, I'll send you to join Talbot and Blackwood in hell!'

His finger tightened on the trigger, and then from behind them a shot rang out!

Jukes staggered, and the expression of his face changed to one of almost ludicrous surprise. His small eyes opened wide, and he stared dazedly into vacancy.

'My God! You've got me, you — ' The

words ended in a choking gasp as the blood welled up into his throat. He swayed once, and then his knees gave way, and he collapsed in a heap on the floor.

Anne, the smoking pistol still clutched in her hand, gave a shrill laugh. Wainwright crossed quickly, and stooped over the motionless form.

'He's quite dead,' he said.

Anne laughed again, a high-pitched hysterical sound.

'I'm glad!' she cried. 'Glad, do you hear? I'd have got him in the end, if it had taken me all my life! He killed Sim — stabbed him without giving him a chance — I didn't give him a chance either, did I? And I saw the fear in his eyes just before he fell. I wouldn't have missed that, it made up a little for the agony I felt when I saw Sim lying there — just where he's lying now — and knew he was dead. I don't care what you do with me now, I'll wait for the detective to come and take me away. I don't care — I don't care — '

Her voice broke, and she fell into a chair sobbing violently.

'Look after her, Elford,' said Wainwright, 'get her some brandy.'

The reporter hurried away, and Wainwright frowned down at the dead man.

'We'll have to swear that she did this in self-defence,' he muttered to John, 'otherwise she'll get into serious trouble, and if she escapes a charge of murder she'll be lucky.'

John nodded and looked at him curiously.

'How did you know all this about Rosher?' he asked. 'Are you connected with the police?'

Wainwright shook his head, and looked at him quizzically.

'No, John,' he said with a smile. 'I'm really — well, I think the best thing you could call me would be the man outside!'

21

The Man Outside

The sound of the shot had wakened the rest of the household, for they heard voices, the noise of opening doors, and footsteps moving about overhead. Presently Peggy appeared at the open door of the library, and looked in with a startled face.

'What was that noise?' she asked, and then as her eyes fell on the huddled thing by the window, she stopped abruptly and drew in her breath sharply.

John Fordyce explained briefly, and she listened in amazement.

'Inspector Jukes!' she breathed. 'It seems ridiculous.'

'It's true all the same,' said Wainwright. 'I don't think you'd better stop in here, it's not very pleasant. Go into the drawing-room and take Anne with you.'

Frank Elford, who had been administering brandy to the still sobbing housemaid, seconded Wainwright's suggestion, and Peggy took Anne away.

'Now,' said Wainwright curtly, 'I'm going to ring up the Chief Constable and tell him what's happened. But before I do that we've got to make up our mind exactly what we're going to say. I suggest that we keep Anne out of this altogether. I'm willing to take the blame for the death of Jukes, and I shall say that we surprised him in the act of trying to steal the emeralds, and that he attacked me. I fired, intending to wound him, and accidentally killed him. Are you game to stick to that story?'

John nodded.

'Right,' said Wainwright, 'well, then, you go and tell the others, so that they know exactly what they've got to say, while I get on to Colonel Hodgkins.'

He had some little difficulty in getting on to the Chief Constable, for he was in bed and asleep, and the exchange had to ring several times before they could get any reply. He listened to what Wainwright had to tell him, and promised to come over as soon as possible. Wainwright hung up the receiver, and made his way to the drawing room.

Anne's threatened fit of hysteria had been warded off, and she was now calm and collected, though a little pale.

'Has Mr. Fordyce told you what we propose to do?' asked Wainwright, and she nodded. 'Then listen,' he went on, 'there's a train from Tor Bridge at seven thirty, which gets into Plymouth at nine. If you catch that, you'll be in time to catch the London train from Plymouth. Now go and pack all your belongings, and have a rest. I'll call you in time, and Elford will drive you in to Tor Bridge.'

She started to thank him, but he cut her short.

'I'm not doing this for your benefit,' he said, 'I'm doing it to save myself a lot of trouble.'

She was going out of the door when John stopped her.

'Have you any money?' he asked.

'Not very much,' she replied, 'only about a couple of pounds.'

'That won't get you very far,' he said.

'Come and see me before you go, and I'll fix it.'

Dawn was breaking before the Chief Constable arrived, red-faced and incredulous. He listened to Wainwright's story and clicked his teeth.

'Well, well,' he said. 'Astounding! Jukes, good God!'

They rang up the police station, and after more delay, an ambulance arrived with a doctor, a constable and a tired sergeant. The doctor made a brief examination, and offered his opinion. The bullet had apparently passed clean through the heart, and the man had died almost instantaneously.

'I'm sorry that I should have done the hangman out of a job,' said Wainwright, 'but it was purely a matter of self-defence, and it couldn't be helped.'

The body was carried down to the ambulance, and it drove away to the little mortuary at Tor Bridge.

Eustace and Georgina, having heard what had occurred, had gone back to bed, to the obvious relief of John, but Peggy and the rest of them made some hot coffee and remained up.

'I expect Superintendent Hanford will get here about ten,' remarked Wainwright, as they sat round the recently-lighted fire in the drawing room, and the Chief Constable, who was in the act of gulping his coffee, looked over the top of his cup with a pair of surprised blue eyes.

'Hanford?' he said. 'Isn't that the Yard man?'

Wainwright nodded.

'What's he coming for?' went on the Chief Constable. 'Who sent for him?'

'I did,' retorted Wainwright. 'Yesterday afternoon.'

Colonel Hodgkins frowned. This flouting of his authority apparently displeased him.

'I think you should have consulted me,' he said gruffly. 'Really you had no right to take matters into your own hands . . . '

'I'm afraid I must differ with you there, Colonel,' answered Wainwright; 'if you will glance at this, you will see my authority for doing what I did.'

He took a card from his pocket, and handed it to the Chief Constable, while the others, with the exception of Elford who knew, looked at him in astonishment.

'God bless my soul!' exclaimed the Colonel. 'I'd no idea. Why didn't you tell me of this before?'

'In the circumstances,' said Wainwright, 'I thought it better that nobody should know.'

'Look here, Harry,' said John, 'isn't it about time you did a little explaining?'

Wainwright pulled out his cigarette case, and lighted a cigarette.

'I suppose it is,' he admitted, blowing out a cloud of smoke. 'Well, I'll start my explanation with an apology. I apologise to you John, and to Peggy, for having lied when I said that my presence here was accidental. It wasn't accidental at all. You see, for the last five years I've held an executive position in the Public Prosecutor's office.'

'Does that mean you're a detective?' demanded John.

'Not exactly,' answered Wainwright. 'But in a sort of way, I suppose I am. My job is to hunt up evidence against people suspected of crime, and that's how I came into this business. If you'll give me some more coffee, I'll tell you the whole story.'

Peggy poured him out another cup, and when he had drunk it he began:

'For a long time the police had been aware that there was a new 'fence' operating. Stories had filtered into the Yard from various sources about a man who bought stolen jewellery in a car at various rendezvous. These places were usually somewhere along a country road, and never in the same spot twice running. They did their level best to try and trap this unknown receiver, but failed through lack of evidence. But they gradually narrowed his operating district down to the vicinity of Princetown. A detective was sent down to nose about, and he became suspicious of Jukes. Jukes was watched, but they couldn't fix anything on him. It isn't difficult to spot a Yard man, particularly when you're in the business yourself, and he probably knew he was being watched, and so stopped all his operations. It was after the 'Duke' Soames business that I was approached.

'Nobody knew me as a detective — for

the simple reason that I'm really not one — and Hanford, who was in charge of the business, had an idea that I might prove more successful than his own men. I was loaned to the Yard, and asked to come down here and see what I could find. Until that moment I hadn't the faintest idea that you and Peggy had come back from the colonies. I knew about Grant, of course, and the emeralds. That is to say, I knew about the robbery at Lowenstein and Marks, and I knew that old William Grant had made all his money through 'fencing'. As a matter of fact, at one time the police strongly suspected him of being the unknown receiver in the car, but they proved that to be wrong, for on the night that 'Duke' Soames sold Lady Conway's pearls the police were watching this house, and old Grant never came out, but that's by the way.

'As I say, I hadn't the faintest idea that you and Peggy were living here, until, talking about Grant, Hanford told me that the old man had been run over, and that his nephew had gone to live in his old house. You could have knocked me down with a feather when he told me the nephew's name, and I realised that it was my old school friend, 'Puddles.'

He paused and flicked the end of his cigarette into the fender.

'It made things very simple for me, you see,' he went on, 'I had to have some sort of a headquarters down here, and I concluded if I appeared in the role of an old acquaintance paying a visit, I was less likely to be suspected. All that rigmarole about being over at Tor Bridge on business, and hearing your name, was, of course, all nonsense. But I didn't want to take anybody into my confidence, and so I pitched the best yarn I could. Well, I hadn't been here very many hours before I heard the story of the man in the drive; the attempt to break in; and the noises in the night. I didn't connect these at all, then, with my own business, and it wasn't until after the murder of Gore, and Elford's identification of him as 'Shiner' Talbot that I began to think that the two things might be intimately connected. I knew, of course that Talbot was responsible for the Bond Street job, and guessed that he had 'fenced' the stuff through Grant. Knowing this, it seemed probable that the emeralds were somewhere in the house, and that it was in search of these that had made Talbot take the position of chauffeur in the name of Gore. There must have been somebody else after the stones, too. That would account for the attempted robbery and the man who was always lurking about in the drive.

'It struck me that this unknown person might very easily be the man I was after, in other words, Jukes. He would have known all about the Bond Street robbery, and the fact that Grant was also a fence. Probably he had, for a long time, suspected that the emeralds were somewhere in the house, since no trace of them had appeared anywhere after they'd been stolen. The arrival of Talbot would have confirmed this suspicion, and it was quite plausible that he should watch Talbot in the hope that he would eventually lead him to the stones. As you know, this theory of mine was the correct one, and there's no need for me to go into details of what happened after. It must all be pretty fresh in your minds.'

He stopped abruptly and lighted another cigarette.

'Where are these emeralds?' asked the Chief Constable.

'Up in my room,' answered Wainwright, 'I'll get them.'

He was gone for less than a minute, and when he came back he carried in his hand a small square parcel.

'Here you are,' he said, untying the string, 'I shall hand them over to Hanford immediately he arrives.'

He unwrapped the paper, and took off the lid of the little box, and then he uttered an exclamation and stared at the contents with dropped jaw. For instead of the emeralds he had expected to see, there was nothing in the box but a handful of bath salts! And then he saw the scrap of paper that had been wrapped round the box with the wrapping — and snatching it up, he read the hastily scrawled pencilled lines. It began without preliminary:

'*I'm sorry to have done this, but I really think that the emeralds are more my property than anybody else's. After all Sim went through, and what I have suffered during the last two days, I'm sure you will agree that I deserve some compensation. Thank you for being so sympathetic, and all that you have done.'*

There was no signature.

'Well I'm damned!' exclaimed Wainwright. 'She's got away with them after all!'

Deaf to the string of questions that followed him, he rushed out of the drawing room, and up the stairs to Anne's room. A glance showed him that it was empty!

When she had gone, he had no idea, but the method of her departure was made clear when later he discovered that his own car was missing from the garage. She must have pushed it down the drive, for they had heard no sound of the engine. A description of Anne and the machine was telephoned to all stations, and during the morning the car was found, abandoned, in a side street near the station at Exeter. But there was no trace of Anne. Both she and the emeralds had vanished, and neither of them was ever found.

'I'm rather inclined to agree with her,' said Wainwright later to Superintendent Hanford, when he explained what had happened. 'I think she did deserve those stones, and after all, I wasn't sent down here to find them. That was a sideline!'

★ ★ ★

Raven House is once more tenantless, its windows, like dead eyes, staring out unseeingly across the bleak moor. The wind blowing round it rustles the ivy, and makes the gaunt trees that line Beech Drive, nod and whisper to each other as they murmur softly of the tragedies they had witnessed.

Neither John nor Peggy could bring themselves to remain in the house after what had happened, and for the time being, they took a furnished flat in London. It was only for the time being, for six months later the girl was married to Frank Elford, and John was left on his own. He need not have been for Georgina suggested that she and Eustace should come and live with him to cheer up his loneliness, but, as he remarked to Wainwright, when the pair of them had dined together one evening:

'I wasn't having any, old man. I might just be able to stand Georgina, on her own, or even Eustace without his mother, but to have the pair of them always with me, I'd rather do twenty years in Dartmoor!'

THE END

We do hope that you have enjoyed reading this large print book.

Did you know that all of our titles are available for purchase?

We publish a wide range of high quality large print books including:
Romances, Mysteries, Classics
General Fiction
Non Fiction and Westerns

Special interest titles available in large print are:
The Little Oxford Dictionary
Music Book, Song Book
Hymn Book, Service Book

Also available from us courtesy of Oxford University Press:
Young Readers' Dictionary
(large print edition)
Young Readers' Thesaurus
(large print edition)

For further information or a free brochure, please contact us at:
Ulverscroft Large Print Books Ltd.,
The Green, Bradgate Road, Anstey,
Leicester, LE7 7FU, England.
Tel: (00 44) **0116 236 4325**
Fax: (00 44) **0116 234 0205**

Other titles in the
Linford Mystery Library:

ECHO OF BARBARA

John Burke

Imprisoned for ten years, Sam Westwood had clung on by remembering his daughter Barbara. Now released, his main desire was to see her. However, Barbara detested her father's memory, and leaving her mother and her brother Roger at home, she had walked out and could not be found. But Roger had his own reason for wanting Barbara back: a wild scheme which, with the addition of Sam's old associates, would prove to have dangerous complications . . .

THE FACELESS ONES

Gerald Verner

An organisation which was so mysterious and vast, its people had been called 'The Faceless Ones'; their file, held by the British Security Service, was labelled 'Group X'. So who are these people — what are their intentions? Magda Vettrilli had found out, but before she could pass on her knowledge, she was shot on the steps of the British Consulate in Tangier. Egerton Scott must discover their identity, and the objective behind 'Group X'. But can he succeed?

THE PURPLE PLAGUE

Derwent Steele

The first victim was a shopkeeper in Bradford. A week later, a publican in Newcastle had collapsed into a coma and later died. Inexorably, similar deaths followed, all in different parts of the country. It appeared that a new form of bacillus was involved. Where had it originated from, how had it arrived into the country, and why did it occur in such diverse places? Dubbed by the press as the 'Purple Plague', was the disease natural? *Or man-made . . . ?*

DARKWATER

V. J. Banis

Jennifer Hale, orphaned and destitute after the Civil War, arrives at Darkwater full of hope, only to be alarmed by her cold reception. More frightening are the screams of Alicia, the dying mistress of the plantation. Jennifer becomes attracted to Walter Dere, her employer, and then Alicia's death frees Walter to propose to her. However, Jennifer develops the symptoms Alicia suffered and remembers Alicia's ravings about witchcraft. Will she suffer a fate worse than death?